MURDER AT THE CASTLE

AN EXHAM-ON-SEA MYSTERY

FRANCES EVESHAM

Boldwood

First published in Great Britain in 2020 by Boldwood Books Ltd.

Cover Design by Nick Castle Design

The characters and events described in the Exham on Sea Mysteries are all entirely fictitious. Some landmarks may strike fellow residents of Somerset, and particularly of Burnham on Sea, as familiar, although liberties have been taken with a few locations.

A CIP catalogue record for this book is available from the British Library.

Paperback ISBN 978-1-80048-032-2

Large Print ISBN 978-1-80048-031-5

Ebook ISBN 978-1-80048-033-9

Kindle ISBN 978-1-80048-034-6

Audio CD ISBN 978-1-80048-038-4

MP3 CD ISBN 978-1-80048-037-7

Digital audio download ISBN 978-1-80048-035-3

Boldwood Books Ltd
23 Bowerdean Street
London SW6 3TN
www.boldwoodbooks.com

1

FRUIT CAKE

Max Ramshore descended the last few steps of the ladder, panting with effort. He dumped a massive cardboard box on the floor, rubbed his back, and sighed. 'How many more boxes are up in your loft?'

Libby chuckled. 'I warned you I had plenty of stuff.'

'You weren't kidding. I thought you downsized when you moved to Exham.'

'You should have seen the amount I threw away. These boxes are full of important items—'

She broke off as Max flipped the lid off the box. 'Soft toys? Really?'

'They belong to Robert.'

'Why are they in your loft and not his?'

Libby wriggled. 'I'm not sure he's told Sarah about them yet.'

'Your son's been married for months. Time for him to confess, I would have thought, and take back his own – er – toys.' Max held aloft a battered tiger. One eye was missing. 'This one's seen action, I suspect, and a ride or two in the washing machine?'

Libby retrieved the toy and slid it gently back into the box.

'Robert promised to come over this afternoon to help me clear the cottage.' She gestured vaguely around the tiny landing. 'He thinks I'm too old and infirm to pack up my own belongings and move to your place...' Her voice faded as she leaned over Max, who'd squatted down to sort through the medley of toys, books, and CD cases. She snatched a soft, blue-covered book from his grasp and flipped it open. 'He used this when he was in primary school. Look, a drawing of his sister.'

'Love Ali's pigtails.'

'She must have been about five when he drew this. He was eight.'

Max laughed. 'Not bad artwork for an accountant.'

Libby stood up. 'Even so, I can't keep everything. I'm making a fresh start when we get married and Robert will have to decide what to do with his belongings. Tell you what, I'll get one of those memory boxes for things I want to keep and the rest is up to him.'

'A small one.'

'Well, medium-sized. If things won't fit, I'll let them go.'

Max pushed the box to one side and set off up the ladder once more.

Libby looked again at the drawing and her stomach flipped. She recognised that stab of anxiety. Ali was grown up and sensible, and Libby liked that she was engaged in voluntary work, but South America seemed so far away.

Even Robert and Sarah's wedding had failed to entice Ali home, and according to her latest email, she wouldn't be back any time soon. She was totally engaged in her voluntary work, and if it weren't for the regular emails she sent home, Libby would suspect she'd lost interest in her family. Would she even get home for Libby's wedding?

Maybe it was Libby's own fault. Determined not to pressure Ali, she'd made light of her wedding, pointing out it was only going to be a quick registry office affair. She'd had quite enough of the 'bells and whistles' approach to matrimony, with her first, deceased, husband, Trevor, and look how that had turned out; he'd been demanding and controlling, and deeply involved in money laundering for a gang of criminals.

No, Libby's second wedding was going to be nothing like the first.

She snapped the book shut and put it back in the box. She wouldn't admit, even to herself, how much she missed her daughter. To stave off the familiar wave of sadness, she slipped into her bedroom to look at her wedding dress. The wedding would be quiet, but it was still an excuse for a new outfit. In knee length navy silk with a pattern of bright red poppies, the dress hung behind the door in a cloud of protective plastic. She'd even bought a hat and red shoes and was planning the cake. Something suitable for an autumn wedding, perhaps, incorporating elderberries.

A contented smile spreading over her face, she shouted up to Max, 'Cup of tea?' and ran down the stairs of the cottage. Bear, the enormous sheepdog, raised his head from the box he shared with Fuzzy, her marmalade cat. He was hoping, as ever, for a titbit. 'No chance. You're starting to get fat.' With a heavy sigh, Bear closed his eyes and went back to sleep.

Shipley, Max's recently adopted springer spaniel, was racing in circles round the garden. Libby hoped he'd work off some of his excess excitement. He'd shown himself to be a talented sniffer dog, and Max was delivering him soon to a specialist trainer, to hone his skills and learn to be calm. Recent attempts to improve his behaviour by attending obedience classes with him had been only mildly effective, and Libby didn't hold out a great deal of hope.

She pottered happily in her kitchen, spooning the tea Max

preferred into a teapot. When she made tea for herself, she stuck lazily to teabags. Opening a cake tin, she cut a hunk of fruit cake, then shaved off a third. Max couldn't resist her home-made cake, and she'd noticed his shirts were just a little tighter over his chest, these days.

Libby leaned on the counter and admired the room. When she was finally installed in Max's old manor house, she'd miss Mandy, her lodger, who planned to stay on for a while, renting the property cheaply while she and Libby continued to run the chocolate business from there. She couldn't bear to leave the professional kitchen, which she'd designed herself. After her husband had died, she'd used up all the money she had, incorporating all the latest kitchen gadgets to help her build up her cake and chocolate business.

Eventually, there would be plenty of room in her new home for an even more splendid workspace. She flipped through a glossy catalogue; one from a pile she'd amassed. Maybe two big ovens, she mused as she delivered tea and cake to Max. But there was no hurry. One step at a time. Marrying Max was more important.

2

COFFEE

Late autumn sun bathed the ancient stones of Exmoor's Dunster Castle in a warm glow. Inside, peace and tranquility reigned. That was just how Margery Halfstead liked it. She shifted a pair of heavy spectacles further up her nose, careful to avoid putting smears on the lenses, and grasped the small, soft brush more firmly. With a satisfied smile, she registered the click of her wedding ring against wood, and breathed in a lungful of slightly musty air.

Surrounded by formidable portraits of other people's ancestors, she felt at home. On the days she worked as a National Trust volunteer, she daydreamed about living in this castle on top of the hill, overlooking the hills and valleys of West Somerset. You could even catch a glimpse of the sea – well, the Bristol Channel – when you looked out of the right windows.

Her husband, William, was here with her today. Humming tunelessly, Margery selected another book from the pile. With a gentle, practised flick of the wrist, she released a year's worth of dust from the top of the pages. The dust motes danced in a random ray of sunlight, finally subsiding invisibly onto the floor. Could there be any better way to spend the day? Margery glanced at William. 'I wonder why dusting old books in a stately home is such fun when...'

'When there's so much housework to do at home,' William finished. They often ended each other's sentences. Hardly surprising, after forty years of marriage. 'Wedded bliss,' William called it.

'Birds of a feather,' her father had called them, years ago.

Margery's brush hovered in the air. She'd often wondered what Father had meant by that.

She gave a mental shrug and carried on with the job. William would never set the world alight, but he'd been a solid, dependable husband. He'd understood his wife's longing for the bigger house they couldn't afford, and he'd put money by. There wasn't enough for a new place, but they were planning an extension. A bigger sitting room, with floor to ceiling windows so Margery could look out on the garden, and one more room upstairs to use for sewing. Mind you, some of the neighbours weren't keen. Mrs Whatshername down the road said she was going to object and stop the planning permission.

William would sort it out. He'd think of a way. Margery rewarded William with a fond smile. Reliability; that's what she liked most about her husband. When you'd known someone for years, you could trust them.

The clatter of heels on wood disturbed the peace as a stranger, a younger woman in her early forties by the look of her, burst in from the passage, gabbling in breathless haste, 'So sorry to butt in. Mrs Moffat, the housekeeper, sent me over here. She said you'd show me the ropes. It's my first day here, you see. I'm Annabel.' She beamed and held out a hand.

Margery suppressed a grimace. She'd raise the issue of proper flat shoes later. Even those ghastly trainers the young people wore would be more suitable than this woman's highly polished, pointy toed boots. She tried to be gracious, putting down the brush to shake the woman's hand. 'You're very welcome, Annabel.' Annabel, what sort of name was that?

William blinked behind horn-rimmed spectacles. 'You'll soon pick things up. I'm William, and this is my wife, Margery. She's the boss when it comes to cleaning.'

The skin tightened on Margery's face; he sounded like a hen-pecked husband. 'William usually shows visitors around the castle, but we're closed between October and February. Just a few pre-arranged groups are allowed.' She shot a glance at her husband. Neither approved of out-of-season tours, for they disturbed the winter peace of the castle.

William wasn't listening. His eyes were on stalks, staring at the stranger. Margery spoke louder. 'A special party of students from the local school will be here shortly. William will lead the tour, but meanwhile...'

'I thought I'd lend a hand with the cleaning,' William cleared his throat. 'Plenty to do.'

Margery nodded. 'The more the merrier.'

'Many hands make light work.'

'No man is an island—' Margery broke off. The newcomer was biting her lip with small white teeth, as though stifling a giggle. Incensed, Margery took a long, slow breath. How dare this newcomer laugh at them?

She narrowed her eyes, summing up Annabel. Almost pretty, except for that snubby nose. Brown hair in a tidy bob, quite suitable. Wide blue eyes, the exact colour of that expensive looking sweater – not cashmere, surely, to come cleaning? A pair of rather expensive, well cut jeans. Margery patted her own fringe into place and sniffed. 'Did they give you an apron?'

Annabel nodded. 'Not that I need it, really. These are my oldest clothes. By the way, Mrs Moffat said you might like a cup of coffee. Can I get you one?'

William looked at the watch Margery gave him last birthday. Nothing too showy – a solid, reliable British watch. He laughed, a little too loud. 'That'll hit the spot, coffee. Can't bring it in here, of course, but I'll come with you, make sure you find the sugar. Are you coming, dear?'

Margery shook her head. 'I'll finish up here. You go on.'

He was already on his way, 'The biscuits are hidden in the cupboard on the right...'

His voice faded away. Margery, alone in the sudden silence, clicked her tongue, replaced the newly dusted book, and reached for another.

* * *

William and Annabel returned, chattering like old friends. Margery flicked a book with harder-than-usual force. Horrified, she watched a page flutter to the floor. She'd never damaged castle property before, not in all the years she'd been volunteering. She shot a wary glance at Annabel, but the younger woman was too busy listening to William telling her about the castle to notice. Margery slipped the page back inside the book.

William hadn't noticed, either. He beamed at his companion, raking a hand through thinning grey hair. Margery remembered when he'd had a blond fringe flopping over his forehead. That was a few years ago, now. Still, he'd aged well.

Annabel's eyes sparkled. 'I'm so excited to be here. I loved history at school, but other things got in the way. Life.'

Curiosity piqued Margery's interest. 'Family?' she suggested.

'Just one son. He's thirteen, now, and it's time I got my life back. I'm a widow, you know. My husband died in a car accident when Jamie was five.' Annabel's hands were clenched.

William's head wagged in sympathy and Margery swallowed. 'That must have been difficult.' She paused. 'Your son must be a great comfort to you.'

Annabel gave a watery smile and started dusting books. 'He is. He's a great kid, but a child's not the same as a husband. I miss his father dreadfully.'

Margery coughed awkwardly, never very comfortable dealing with personal matters. How could she know what to say? 'Now, it's time for you to let these students in, William. Goodness knows why Mrs Moffat made a special arrangement, just for them.' She sniffed. 'Something about history exams, I think you said?'

'Quite right, dear, but I can't stand here all day. We're starting off in the modern butler's pantry, so the students can try out the speaking tube.' A favourite feature of the castle, the tube allowed the butler to speak to kitchen staff, downstairs in the servants' quarters. 'Then, I'll take them round the rest of the castle, finishing with a Victorian tea party later. Mrs Forest will be bringing a cake.'

Margery hesitated, every vestige of her earlier contentment destroyed by Annabel's arrival. She wouldn't spend any more time with this superior younger woman if she could help it. She replaced her brush in its bag. 'I'll give my husband a hand, if you're happy to carry on here.' She'd be glad to join the tour, and some of Libby Forest's cake would be just the job to cheer her up.

* * *

Heaving teenage bodies filled the tiny butler's pantry. They shuffled, giggled and – Margery sniffed the air – passed wind. She wrinkled her nose. A tall lad, towering over his companions, disproportionate height miraculously supported by a skeletal frame, bent over to place his mouth against the speaking tube and affected an exaggerated upper class accent. 'Hello. Who's there? I'm talking on behalf of Mr Haddock, the butler. To whom am I speaking?'

A distant, tinny voice filled the room. 'Elsie 'ere. I'm the scullery maid.'

William hissed in the lad's ear, 'Use your script.'

Face pink as he struggled with self-conscious giggles, the youth pulled a crumpled sheet of lined paper from his pocket. 'I'd like to speak to the cook.'

The voice replied, 'Ooh, she's out, I'm afraid. Can I 'elp, at all?'

Margery raised an eyebrow. She knew that voice. Beryl Nightingale, a fellow volunteer, was a timid little woman, not someone Margery would have chosen for an acting role. She supposed William thought he was doing Beryl a favour. Maybe he was right. Beryl sounded unusually confident today.

As the student continued to read from his script, William hissed at Margery. 'I've left some handouts in the car. Can you take over here? Send everyone downstairs to the old Victorian kitchen when they're finished here. I'll do the tour of the castle afterwards. I've given them maps.'

'B-but,' Margery wanted to argue. She hated dealing with visitors, and schoolchildren were the worst of all, but she was too late. William had already gone.

The teenager, enjoying himself, went on speaking through the tube. 'Mr Haddock, the butler, wishes to confirm tonight's dinner menu.'

The menu was almost lost in his companions' gleeful snorts. Margery could hear Beryl listing elaborate dishes, from partridge soup and potted crayfish to scotch woodcock. She began to think the catalogue would never end. Beryl was relishing the starring role. Finally, the litany came to an end, '... and queen of pudd—'

The disembodied voice fell abruptly silent. The young man shouted into the speaking tube. 'Hello. Are you there?'

More silence.

Margery stepped forward. 'It gets blocked sometimes. Try blowing into the tube.'

The boy puffed and the device produced a loud raspberry, but there was no reply. The scullery maid, it seemed, had gone.

'Right, never mind.' Margery swallowed. She wasn't good at handling groups of students. They made her nervous. She tapped one of the boys on the shoulder. 'You come upstairs with me. You can tug the bell-pull while the rest go down to the servants' quarters, find the row of bells on the wall, and wait. Mr Halfstead will join you there.'

'Will they ring downstairs? Like in Downton Abbey?'

'Exactly.'

Margery climbed towards the bedrooms, an excited teenager in tow. Her knees ached.

As one foot reached the landing, a single cry rang through the castle. Another volunteer, a big woman, poked her head out from a nearby doorway. Neat black hair framed her face. Her blouse was printed with bright swirls that made Margery's head spin. 'What's that?'

'Party of schoolchildren.'

Another cry interrupted. The two women's eyes met. Without another word, Margery turned and, forgetting her painful knees, ran down the stairs to the servants' quarters.

She burst through into the old kitchen, the young lad close behind. William was already there, bent over, peering behind the huge metal-topped table that dominated the room.

out. 'It's enough trouble dealing with the three we have between us, plus the dogs. And Fuzzy, of course. Mustn't forget the cat, even if she does spend all day in your airing cupboard at the moment. I hope she finds mine as desirable.'

'Anyway.' Libby was firm. 'If you'll look after the dogs this morning, I'll get the cake over to Dunster Castle and be back for lunch. Then you can deliver Shipley to the trainer.' The cake was another reason for leaving the dogs at home. Three layers, iced, with a Victorian-style sugar pineapple perched on top – what was this Victorian thing about pineapples? The sweet smell alone would drive the dogs crazy, quite apart from the health and safety issues of letting animals anywhere near her catering.

'Ah, lunch.' Max rubbed his stomach. 'By the way, I found some fishing tackle in your loft. Robert's, I suppose?'

'Not mine, that's for sure. Did you want it?'

'No, but seeing it made me think. There's a local club. We used to have competitions, but it all got a bit nasty. You won't remember, because it was just before you arrived in Exham, but there was some bad feeling. People accused of weighting the scales.'

'Really? Why would anyone care that much about fishing?'

'You'd be surprised. I just thought I might take it up again.'

Libby laughed. 'Good idea. It'll keep you out from under my feet. Isn't that what old married couples say?'

She climbed into the car and waved goodbye through the open window as she rounded the corner into the road, watching in the mirror as Max and the dogs vanished from view. The mirror reflected her ridiculous grin. Contentment. That's what she felt. It had taken her months – years, almost – to realise marrying Max would not necessarily mean loss of independence. She was embarrassed to remember how she'd dithered and hesitated, and done her best to drive Max away. At last, recognising she'd lose him if she didn't make up her mind, she'd proposed to him.

They'd made plans for the ceremony and given notice to the registry office, so they could marry whenever they chose. There was no hurry. Her son Robert's wedding had ended in drama, but Libby was determined to have as quiet an event as possible, and Max hated any kind of fuss. He had breathed a sigh of relief. 'If you're sure that's what you want, it will suit me fine. We'll go to the registry office on our own and do the deed. They'll supply witnesses.'

'For the first time in my life,' Libby had confided to her friend, Angela, 'I don't feel under any pressure to do what other people want me to. I'm free, at last.'

Angela, long a widow, had looked wistful. As Libby drove, she mentally ran through a list of men she knew, wondering if any would be suitable for her friend. Oliver, perhaps, who'd been at school with Max? Or Reg, the African American basketball player who came over to Exham at every opportunity. He'd dallied with Libby's apprentice and lodger, Mandy, but that relationship had fizzled out. Reg was in his thirties, about halfway between Mandy and Angela, but maybe Angela would like a toy boy?

A ray of sunshine broke through the late autumn clouds, adding to Libby's glow of well-being. Her own happiness made her want the same for everyone but she'd try not to interfere in other people's lives. She had enough to think about with the cake and chocolate business, and the private investigation partnership she'd established with Max. Angela would have to find her own way forward.

Libby changed gear. On the other hand, it would be nice to see Angela happy. Perhaps she could try on-line dating?

The purple Citroen screeched to a standstill. Dunster Castle was in uproar. A police car, blue lights flashing, blocked the driveway as white-clad figures moved purposefully around the entrance, securing police tape across the road.

Libby recognised a crime scene when she saw one. She climbed out of the Citroen, leaving the cargo of cake, keen to find out more, only to hear a harsh voice. 'Wait there.' The familiar, unwelcome, figure of Police Constable Ian Smith levered an over-weight body from the front seat of the police car.

His small eyes were screwed into pinpricks of malevolent light and Libby's heart sank. He'd never liked her. For one thing, she'd succeeded in solving several murder investigations, leaving PC Smith and his colleagues with egg on their faces. Some in the police force had slowly grown used to having Libby around, and afforded her a reasonable measure of respect. It had helped that Max's background as a financial consultant, often working for the government, was valuable to the local police service. Recently, as Libby and Max's standing as private investigators gained traction, they'd been invited to undergo a trial period working for the increasingly stretched police force. They were rather grandly described as civilian investigating officers. What's more, they were paid for their work.

PC Smith disagreed profoundly with a policy of allowing 'muggles' anywhere near investigations. 'Sorry, Mrs Forest. Not this time.' He looked as though he could hardly speak civilly to Libby.

'Actually, I have my official badge with me.'

She kept her voice friendly and tried hard not to look smug as she pulled out the laminated card, but Smith's lip curl made it plain she'd failed. 'You're not involved in this one yet.'

Libby's pulse quickened. Not involved yet? So, she was likely to be? Her stomach lurched and she drew a sharp breath at the familiar mix of excitement and foreboding. 'Might not even be a murder,' he continued. 'The old woman probably had a heart attack after walking up that road.' He pointed up the steep slope that led towards the castle's thirteenth century gateway.

'Someone's dead?'

PC Smith folded his arms across a beer gut. His face flushed red. Clearly, he'd given away more information than he intended, so keen to put Libby in her place he'd forgotten to watch his tongue. 'They won't let you in to the scene,' he grumbled.

Libby stepped round him, wondering how he'd ever managed to pass a fitness assessment. 'We'll see.'

She climbed through the gateway and up a flight of steps, arriving breathless at the entrance to the castle. Detective Sergeant Joe Ramshore, Max's son, ducked under the yellow police tape to greet her, pulling off white gloves on the way. 'Well, news really travels fast around here. Nice to see you, step-mother-to-be. Is your partner-in-crime here too?'

'Not today. Max is involved in some of these bitcoin mining frauds. He spends most of his time tracking down computer viruses, trying to find their source. It's going to take weeks, if not months. Some of his old government contacts sent the work his way, and as you can imagine, he's loving it.'

Joe laughed. 'That sounds like him. Never happier than gazing at a screen, fingers on the keyboard. Rather him than me. But what brought you to our latest crime scene? Are you developing second sight or did someone tip you off?'

'Pure coincidence. I'm here on bakery business, delivering cake for a group of visiting schoolchildren, though it looks as though they won't be eating it. What's up?'

'Elderly lady dead in the kitchens.'

'Anyone I know?'

Joe clicked his tongue. 'I'm afraid so. Beryl Nightingale. She belongs – well – belonged to the Exham on Sea History Society. Was she one of your friends?'

Libby had not known it was possible to feel colour drain from your own face. She'd been a member of the society since she arrived in the area, so she knew Beryl. Last time Libby saw her, the older woman had perched like a small brown sparrow on a wooden chair, nibbling on cake crumbs and whispering with her old friends, George Edwards and the Halfsteads. 'Beryl? Not really? What – I mean how did she die?'

'We don't know if it's natural causes yet, or something more sinister. It could be a stroke or heart attack. There's no obvious sign of foul play, but we'll wait to hear from the pathologist.'

He made a wry face. 'Unfortunately, we have a gaggle of schoolkids here, and if I'm not mistaken they'll already have texted the whole of Somerset with lurid gossip, so our friends in the press will arrive at any moment.'

He paused to take a deep breath, before finishing with a dramatic flourish. 'What's more, one of the boys is that new local member of parliament's son.'

Libby's mouth formed a soundless whistle. 'An MP? Now, that's going to cause some complications, if Beryl's death turns out to be anything other than natural causes.'

'Sure will. What's more, the lad was talking to Beryl when she had her seizure, or whatever it was. His dad's not going to like it.' Joe raised his eyes to the heavens. 'Tell you what, if you want to sit in on young Jason Franklin's initial interview, I could use your input. In your new official capacity.'

* * *

Jason Franklin's long, bony body perched on a wooden chair in one of the offices at the back of the castle, well away from the public areas. His arms and legs, sticking out at odd angles, reminded Libby of the spider her son had once kept as a pet, against Libby's better judgement. She'd always hated the beast, shuddering every time she passed the tank in his bedroom. Robert insisted spiders were harmless. Libby did not believe him.

The boy's uniform marked him out as a pupil at the local comprehensive school. The regulation tight grey trousers failed to quite cover bare ankles, and he wore no socks. Did young people not feel the cold? Whether the shortness of the trousers was due to a teenage growth spurt or simply current fashion, Libby had no idea.

Jason's intelligent, sharp featured face was alight. Excitement or nerves? He waved his hands in the air as his voice veered between a deep, adult brown tone and occasional adolescent crackles.

A young detective constable, neat in black trousers and jumper, with long fair hair tied in a ponytail, sat opposite Jason, nodding at his answers. She looked up as Libby entered, her face blank. Recognition dawned and her expression hardened. 'Mrs Forest. Can I help?'

Libby's heart sank at the sight of another resentful police officer. What had she done to annoy this one? They hadn't met, before today. She fixed a friendly smile on her face and held up her pass. 'DS Ramshore wants me to sit in, if that's OK, Detective Constable?'

The young officer raised an eyebrow, and Libby's spirits dropped further. She was not welcome here.

A police radio crackled, and the young detective constable fiddled with it for a few seconds before she spoke. Her otherwise pleasant voice held a hard edge as she spoke. 'Very well. I'm Detective Constable Gemma Humberstone. There's tea and coffee over there.' She nodded to a tray on a nearby table. 'Jason is just explaining what happened. Of course, this is only to get a feel of things. If we need to talk more, we'll organise an appropriate adult to be with us, as Jason is a minor.' Libby nodded. The detective constable clearly intended to proceed according to the book. Well, that made a refreshing change from PC Ian Smith's slap-dash methods.

Libby tilted the coffee pot over a cup. Liquid dribbled out, the colour of treacle. It must have been brewing for some time. Preferring not to give herself palpitations, Libby took another cup and used a teabag instead.

The DC raised her voice. 'Now, this is just a preliminary chat, as I was saying, Jason.' Libby caught the implied rebuke and subsided quietly into her seat, sipping lukewarm tea. DC Humberstone continued. 'You were all together in the butler's pantry?'

The boy nodded. 'We were – I was – talking into the speaking tube. It goes from the butler's pantry to the kitchens. Everyone was there. I mean, all of us from school.'

He paused, and the DC waited, but he said no more. She asked, 'Did you have a teacher with you?'

'No. Mr Halfstead was in charge. He works here. I think he's a course leader, or something.' DC Humberstone nodded and made a note as he talked. 'There were a couple of other people as well. People who work here, I think. I'm not really sure.'

'Don't worry. We'll get names and so on before people leave. Just tell me what you remember. In your own words.'

The teenager scratched at his chin, leaving a pink mark. 'Well, nothing much. I mean, like, I asked her what was on the menu for dinner – pretending to be part of the staff, you see.' He screwed his eyes shut, obviously trying to be precise. 'She talked about food – different courses – one was something called a shape. I was going to ask her what that was, but I didn't get a chance. She gave a sort of hiccup and stopped talking.' He frowned. 'I wasn't really worried, and Mrs Halfstead didn't seem too bothered, anyway. She sent us down to the servants' hall and then she took one of the others up to the bedrooms to ring a bell. They have this full set of bells on the wall, like in the servants' quarters, so the family can summon help when they need it...'

His voice faded away. 'We didn't know what had happened. We all ran down the stairs. Mr Halfstead was already there. He turned and shouted at us to stay where we were, but we'd already seen what looked like a bundle of rags on the floor. Someone screamed, I think.' He shrugged. 'I didn't see the lady's face, just a bit of her skirt and that. It was all a muddle, with people shouting.'

'Did anyone try to revive the lady?'

'I think he did – Mr Halfstead, I mean. He bent over her, like he was giving her mouth to mouth.'

'OK. That's fine, Jason.'

As DC Humberstone rose, Libby put in, 'Do you mind if I ask a question, Jason?' She ignored the DC's cold stare. 'Can you tell me exactly what you said to Ber— I mean, to Miss Nightingale, through the speaking tube?'

He reached inside his back pocket. 'I had a script. Here.' He hesitated, then offered it to Libby.

To avoid further antagonising DC Humberstone, Libby shook her head. The police officer held out a plastic bag and Jason slipped the sheet of paper inside. Libby would have a chance to scrutinise it later. 'Did you write this yourself?'

'With my mates. We had a session at school about coming here today. Mr Halfstead gave us a talk on the history of the castle and that, and then we wrote down what we'd say.'

'Just one more thing,' Libby asked, feeling the atmosphere in the room, already chilly, cool by several degrees under the detective constable's continued disapproval. 'Why were you the one talking through the tube? I mean, how were you chosen?'

Jason beamed, and for the first time, Libby caught a glimpse of his personality as pride overcame his shock. 'I won it in a competition.'

'A competition? Organised by...'

'Mr Halfstead.'

4

SHORTBREAD

For the first time, Libby was allowed into the Incident Room in the police station, a sign of her new status as an official adjunct to the police. Joe Ramshore led the way, pushed open the door and stood back to let her in. Libby looked round the room, her heart sinking at the sight of PC Ian Smith, leaning against a wall. His eyes had narrowed to virtual invisibility and his upper lip curled in a sneer. By his side sat DC Humberstone. She glanced round at Libby, then turned back, her face stony.

Joe made the introductions. 'Some of you already know Libby Forest. She helped with the recent murder case over at the bridge in West Somerset, and DCI Morrison's asked her to work with us on this case. We can use her in the investigation, but you need to remember she's a civilian. DCI Morrison will be here soon, and he's keen we welcome her properly.'

Libby felt her face burn as PC Smith snorted, loud enough for her to hear. 'Always around when there's a suspicious death, isn't that right, Mrs Forest? Anyone would think you know it's coming.' Another officer slurped a mouthful of coffee and sniggered.

Joe raised a hand. Before he could come to her defence, Libby stepped forward. She needed to stand up for herself. 'I help when I can.' She took a breath. 'I've brought cake.' Someone made an appreciative noise as she pulled the tin from her over-sized tote bag. 'This was intended for the school party at the castle. They won't need it now, and I thought you might like some. Oh, and some shortbread.'

The coffee drinking constable took the tin, opened the lid, and sniffed. 'Smells OK. What's this pineapple on the top for?'

Libby followed him to a side table. 'It's part of a Victorian theme. The students intended to visit the old Victorian kitchen and the Victorians were fond of pineapples – something about one-upmanship if you could grow them in your orangery.' The constable cut a huge slice, swallowed it in two bites, and murmured through a mouthful of crumbs, 'Not bad.' Libby had a theory that when people eat food you've cooked, they feel obliged to be civil, at least. So far, so good.

The door opened. 'Right, if you've all finished stuffing your faces, let's get on.' Detective Chief Inspector Morrison had arrived. Libby had met the senior officer several times before. His deeply lined face wore the crestfallen expression of a man who expected very little from the world and was seldom disappointed. Nevertheless, his reputation for clearing up crime on his patch brought grudging respect, even from the likes of PC Smith.

The detective chief inspector opened the discussion. 'We don't have a report yet from the pathologist but he gave a few hints. First thoughts about the cause of death are unclear. No wounds of any sort. The victim appeared to be alone in the kitchen, by the speaking tube. There's no chair, so she must have been standing, which suggests she felt well. Not much more to tell, at this stage, I'm afraid.'

The crime scene manager, a short, cheerful woman wearing baggy black trousers and solid, flat shoes, described police activities at the unusual scene. 'This may not be a crime scene, but given the deceased lady's good health and a few preliminary thoughts from the pathologist, we decided to treat the death as suspicious and collect as much forensic evidence as possible.'

She glanced at Libby. 'We don't want to dismiss this as natural causes and look like fools.' That had happened more than once in the past couple of years.

'Unfortunately, dozens of people visit the Victorian kitchen every day, so finger marks are not likely to lead us anywhere, unless we take prints from everyone who's visited the castle this year.'

Someone groaned. 'We won't be going down that route yet, not without extra resources,' DCI Morrison confirmed. 'Do we have any other leads?'

'We're testing the victim's possessions. She's not allowed to have a handbag with her in the castle, apparently, but she had a few things in her apron pockets. Nothing very interesting. Mints, purse, a diary with very few entries – the usual things. Plus, some personal souvenirs – a small silver photograph album, the kind that takes just two photos, and a hip flask. One picture is of an old lady bearing a very strong resemblance to the victim – perhaps a relative – and the other is of a young man. That photo's in black and white, and judging from the lad's clothes and haircut, a proper short back and sides with a neat parting, it was taken back in the fifties. We may get something useful from them.'

DC Gemma Humberstone and PC Ian Smith reported on their initial conversations with the volunteers and schoolboys. Most had been brief, placing people at various points around the castle. All accounts confirmed that Beryl Nightingale was alone in the kitchen.

Libby shut her eyes for a moment and imagined the scene. Beryl, who'd so often longed to take centre stage in the history

society meetings, must have been thrilled with her starring role
in the little drama. She could never have dreamed it was about to
end so tragically.

DCI Humberstone displayed the sheet of A4 the schoolboy
had handed over, still encased in its protective plastic bag. 'This is
Jason's script. He was reading it as he spoke to Beryl Nightingale
through the butler's tube. He took the main part in their little
drama, after a competition organised by William Halfstead.
That's the Halfstead who discovered the body. We took his statement at the scene.'

Ian Smith said, 'Sounds like a suspect, to me.' The cake eating
officer, a young man with spiky hair and the pink face of someone
who hardly needs to shave, nodded, but DCI Morrison held up a
warning hand.

'Now, let's not jump to conclusions. At this stage, we ask questions: who, what, when, how, where and why. We need to know
everything about the key witnesses. Remember, although we may
have suspicions, we don't even know yet if this is a murder. We're
still waiting for confirmation from the pathologist.' He turned to
Libby. 'Mrs Forest, you knew the victim. One of your history
society members, I'm told. What can you tell us about her?'

Libby's neck tingled as she tried to think, conscious of every
eye on her. 'The society stopped meeting over the summer. The
next discussion's due in a couple of days, as it happens, so I
haven't seen Beryl there for a while.' She remembered something,
'She's been coming to the bakery more often than usual, recently,'

'Any reason why, so far as you know?'

'I'm not sure.' Libby thought back to a remark heard in the
shop. 'I think she recently retired. I'm hoping to find out more
about her at the meeting. Some of the members have known her
for years. She's always been so quiet.' She wracked her brain for
ways to describe Beryl, but the woman's personality had been so

withdrawn Libby hardly knew her. 'She likes carrot cake.' PC Smith's lip curled in a sneer and Libby stopped talking, annoyed at sounding unprofessional. They didn't need to know that sort of gossip.

DCI Morrison followed the direction of her gaze. 'Ian. You have something to add?'

PC Smith folded his arms across his chest and stared at the floor like a sulky child. 'No, sir.'

The DCI nodded, tasked a couple of officers with taking full statements from the volunteers at the castle, and set a date for the next conference. 'But, before you all go, I have an announcement. DS Ramshore will be leaving us. He's passed his exams – not before time, I might add.' He scowled with mock severity at Joe. 'He's moving on to West Mercia as a detective inspector.'

5

SALMON

That afternoon, Shipley's absence on a few days training made Max's house seem eerily quiet. 'I'm looking forward to his return as a reformed character,' Max said. 'In the meantime, let's give Bear some exercise. There's an hour or two before the light goes. He can have our full attention, for once.'

They headed for Brent Knoll, one of the peculiar rounded Somerset hills that rise from the Levels as landmarks, visible for miles around. The unseasonable warm weather of the past few days had faded. Libby shivered. 'The nights are drawing in, fast.'

Max stopped, drew in a huge lungful of air, and stretched his arms towards the sky. 'I love this time of year. I like wearing cosy clothes, there's a hint of melancholy, the trees have finished turning, and there's the promise of Christmas just around the corner.'

Libby's spirits rose. 'We'll be an old married couple by then.'

Max slid his arm round her shoulders, pulled her close, and kissed her. 'Now, do you feel warmer?'

She drew back to study Max's face, tracing with her finger the laughter lines round his eyes and the dent in his chin, all as familiar, now, as her own features. She leaned in again, drinking in his warm, masculine scent and the sharp hint of aftershave, recognising it as one of her presents to him.

'Why are you laughing?' Max asked.

'Because I'm happy. And astonished at my good luck.' She'd arrived in Exham on Sea, released by widowhood from an unhappy marriage, never expecting to find real love at this late stage of life.

Bear, who'd been trotting ahead, stopped dead. He hesitated, then bounded over and reared up on his hind legs, aiming his wet tongue at Libby's face. The romantic spell was broken and Max let her go. 'He's jealous.'

'Come on, Bear.' Laughing, Libby chased ahead, Bear matching his pace to hers. Before long, she had to admit defeat, gasping, 'That dog could keep going for hours.'

'It's the breed. His ancestors travelled miles, watching sheep on the Carpathian hills.'

Bear, tail aloft with pleasure, turned his attention to sniffing at hedgerows. Max asked, 'How did the police conference go?'

Libby kicked at a stone. 'Not brilliant, if I'm honest. Some of the officers think I'm just playing at investigations. They don't want me, especially now Joe is moving on. I'm pleased for him, of course, but things could be tricky.' Suddenly furious, she burst out, 'They think I'm an impostor, no matter how many cases I solve. They believe I should stick to the chocolate business.'

Max nodded and walked on a few paces, deep in thought. 'It's not surprising some of the – well, the less enlightened among the police resent you. They feel threatened, because you've been the one catching murderers. They're not all so inflexible. DCI Morrison wants you there. He thinks a great deal of you.'

It was true, Morrison gave every sign of listening when Libby spoke. She kicked through a pile of fallen leaves. 'I wish Ian

Smith didn't dislike me so much, and Gemma Humberstone's almost as frosty.'

'They'll get used to you. The sensible ones will see you're good at your job, although I fear Ian Smith might never get it. He's a lost cause, but that's his problem. If justice was left to the likes of him, it would never be done.'

'You're right. It's almost as if his attitude has affected the others, so the best way to prove myself is by finding out what happened to Beryl. Morrison believes her death's suspicious, at the very least. I'm sure the pathologist would have recognised a stroke or heart attack straight away. Suicide seems unlikely, given she was in the middle of a conversation.'

Libby paused as a familiar mix of excitement and horror kicked in once more. That feeling never failed to grab hold at the beginning of a new case. With a burst of determination, she announced, 'I won't let Ian Smith and his childish buddies intimidate me. Besides, I owe it to Beryl to get justice, if she was murdered.' She walked faster. 'I'm back on the case, Max, which is just as well. You're too busy to work on this one, but it helps to talk it through.'

'And that's why we're a team.'

Libby's brain clicked into gear. 'Let's think. Why would anyone want to kill a helpless old lady like Beryl?'

'That's the puzzle,' said Max. 'How much do we know about her?'

'Hardly anything. She's like people's old aunts. You know, always there on the side-lines, but no one takes any notice of them. They don't seem to matter, not in the rush of day-to-day life. I hardly knew her, although she was always at the history society meetings. She never said much, just sat in the corner, eating cake, waiting to be asked to give a talk about her ancestors.

I don't know much about her background. Do you? You grew up in Exham.'

He shook his head. 'Not really, though I knew the name. I was more interested in football than middle-aged spinsters, and our paths never crossed, but I can tell you who will know all the detail.'

'Go on, then, who?'

'Your friend, Angela. She's known Beryl all her life.'

'Of course.' Angela Miles, born and bred in Exham, knew the history of everyone in the area. 'You're right. I'll talk to her tomorrow. Then, the rest of the society's getting together in a couple of days. I should get some useful background from them.'

Max stopped at a railway bridge and leaned on the wall, watching for trains. 'While you're in this positive mood, how about setting a date for the wedding?'

'Mm.' Libby thought of the dress, hanging patiently in her cottage, and her belongings all packed in boxes. 'Let's do it soon.'

'How soon?'

Libby tried to analyse her feelings. What was holding her back? She was dying to get married to this man. She loved everything about him, even his fondness for poring over a computer for hours at a time. Moving into his manor house and learning to call it home felt like an adventure, so why was she hesitating? She pictured a wedding, bigger than the one they were planning, surrounded by their children – Robert and Joe, with their wives, Shipley, and Bear, of course, but something was missing. 'Ali,' she murmured. 'I wish Ali could be there.'

A train thundered past, shaking the bridge under their feet, drowning Max's response.

'What did you say?' Libby asked.

'I said, have you asked your daughter to come?'

'I mentioned it, but I know she can't come all the way from

Brazil, just for my wedding.' Ali was happy and her voluntary work was worthwhile, even though, according to her emails, she was permanently broke.

'I'm being silly. Let's not wait. How about two weeks on Saturday?'

'Perfect.' Max landed a kiss on her cheek and set off at a run. 'Meanwhile, race you to Brent Knoll.'

* * *

Libby spent the evening in her cottage, packing. Now they'd set a date for the wedding, there was plenty to do. Libby checked she had ample supplies of coffee so the cottage would smell enticing when they arrived. She'd bake bread, as well. If that didn't sell the house, nothing would.

Fuzzy, her aloof marmalade cat, reacted to Libby's return with a cold stare. She deigned to nibble at a tiny mouthful of the best salmon, stalked from the room, and returned to the airing cupboard to curl up in her favourite spot. She was an aging cat, almost sixteen, and her muzzle displayed a mix of original ginger and grey fur. 'Oh, Fuzzy, don't you go getting old. I couldn't manage without you.' With a sudden overwhelming rush of emotion, Libby plucked the cat from her nest on a pile of recently ironed duvet covers and buried her face in the soft fur.

Like all cats, Fuzzy despised unnecessary emotion. She struggled out of her owner's arms, but allowed Libby to stroke her back as she settled back to sleep, warm and happy. 'Sometimes I wish I was a cat,' Libby muttered. 'Life would be much simpler.'

She worked fast, for once unhindered by the attentions of the dogs. The process was far easier in their absence. Only the other day, Shipley had stolen one of Libby's favourite red sandals, sloped off to a corner, and chewed the leather to shreds.

With half the contents of her house neatly packed in boxes, Libby sank into a chair, exhausted, to watch the news on television. She hardly heard a word; her brain was too full of Beryl. Why would anyone want to harm such a gentle soul? Unmarried, Beryl had led a quiet, solitary life. Libby had arranged to visit Angela the next day. With luck, her friend would share a few details.

Libby sighed, switched off the TV set, and made a cup of hot chocolate, ignoring the automatic pang of guilt. She'd walked a long way with Max, so she had calories to spare. A few mouthfuls of chocolate wouldn't stop her fitting into the wedding dress.

As she sipped, guiltily savouring the drink's sweet richness, her phone rang. The caller ID was blocked, so it was probably the police. Maybe the news would be good.

'Mrs Forest, it's Detective Constable Gemma Humberstone here.' There was an edge of excitement in the DC's voice that set Libby's heart pumping.

'I'm sorry to call so late, but DCI Morrison wanted you to know as soon as possible—'

'Yes?' Breathless, Libby cut her short. 'Know what?'

'The pathologist telephoned again. He won't entirely commit himself yet, but he's pretty sure Beryl Nightingale died from nicotine poisoning.'

6

HOT CHOCOLATE

Libby's hot chocolate cooled, untouched, as she scoured the
internet for everything she could find on nicotine poisoning. It
was past midnight before she slept, but the next morning she rose
early, watching the time tick slowly past. She forced herself to
wait until a reasonable hour before she locked the cottage and set
off to visit Angela.

Her friend looked charming and elegant as always. Even in
the early morning, her hair shone and subtle makeup brightened
her face. Libby had tried, but she could never match Angela's
easy style.

She welcomed Libby graciously with freshly brewed coffee
and a plate of Libby's own shortbread. 'I think you're one of my
best customers,' Libby pointed out. 'How do you stay so slim?'

'Genes. I can't help it, I was born lucky. My mother lived to be
ninety-five, and I'm planning to last even longer.' Angela flicked
an invisible speck of dust from the coffee table. 'Now, what did
you want to ask me about? I'm sorry you had to make a special
journey, by the way. I know you're meeting the rest of the history
society, but I've promised to go over to Wells Cathedral for an

extra session tomorrow. They have more visitors than ever, these days.' Angela worked as a guide, showing sightseers round the building. She pulled a face. 'I wonder whether there's a degree of notoriety adding to visitors' interest, ever since – you know – that awful business.'

Libby shot her friend a sharp glance, diverted for a few minutes from the purpose of her visit. Her inbuilt detection systems were on the alert. Angela had not seemed so lively for months, not since she was involved in the murder at the cathedral. 'Come on. What's happened to cheer you up? Something special – or someone?'

Angela beamed. 'I'm not sure, yet. I'll tell you in a while. It might all fizzle out.' She made a show of crossing her fingers. 'But, you didn't come to talk about my social life. I imagine you need to discuss Beryl.'

'You're right. I'll let it go for now, but you're not off the hook. I'll be back! I hope things work out.'

'If I end up half as happy as you and Max, I'll be delighted. By the way, I haven't forgiven you for wanting a tiny wedding with no guests.'

Libby grinned. 'Maybe we can make an exception for you.'

Libby pulled out a battered spiral pad and a pen. Taking notes helped to draw a line between friendship and investigating. 'I need to know everything about Beryl. Her life story, if you can fill in the details. You never know what may be important. I'm working officially with the police on this case. DCI Morrison's teams are collecting the hard evidence, forensics and so on, but they've asked me to gather general information from people who knew Beryl. As her only interest seems to have been the history society, and volunteering at Dunster Castle, I'll be talking to all the members, to hear background details.' She paused, anticipating the effect of the announcement she was about to make. 'Beryl died from nicotine poisoning.'

Angela's eyebrows shot up. 'Nicotine? You mean, from cigarettes? But, she didn't smoke.' She frowned. 'Was it an accident, or – or something even worse?'

'I'm afraid either accident or suicide is unlikely. It would be an odd way to kill herself, and if she didn't smoke...' Libby explained the few facts she'd learned. 'It's not difficult to distil the poison from cigarettes, but there would be plenty of easier ways to do away with yourself. It's been used in the past for murder, though, because cigarettes are easily accessible in large numbers. Beryl must have eaten or drunk something tasting strong enough to disguise the nicotine.'

Angela's eyes were stretched wide, her face horrified. 'Who would do such a thing to Beryl? And why?' she whispered. She fell silent, rolling the hem of her jumper between agitated fingers. She opened her mouth, then closed it again while Libby waited, sure her friend had something important to say.

After a moment, Angela leaned forward. 'I don't like to tattle about Beryl, especially now she's dead. You know, never speak ill...' Her voice trailed away.

Libby nodded encouragement. 'It's so important to find out all I can about her. If she had secrets, they may be the reason she was killed. In any case, whatever you know will help.'

Angela wrinkled her nose. 'I'm sure you're right, and you'll probably find out from someone else. You see, Beryl had a secret. She – well – she had an occasional drink or two. Alone. During the day. In fact, I suppose you could say she was almost an alcoholic.'

Libby bit her lip to hide disbelief. Mousy Beryl? Surely not? Then, she remembered that the police had found a silver hip flask in Beryl's bag. She let her breath out in a long sigh. Perhaps Angela was right. 'What did she drink?'

'Well, I believe she's been seen with a supermarket trolley full of bottles of whisky.'

Libby ran a finger round the rim of her cup, thinking it through. 'A good slug of whisky would mask the taste of nicotine.'

The two friends stared at one another. Angela winced. 'There's quite a story to Beryl, I'm afraid. Oh dear. I hate to gossip even more...'

Libby let the pause lengthen, allowing her friend to gather her thoughts. Eventually, Angela leaned forward, replaced her bone china plate on the polished occasional table by her elbow, and gave a small shake of the head. 'I can see you need to know the full story, to understand what made Beryl tick. It's a sad tale, and it goes back a long way.'

Libby scribbled fast as Angela talked. 'Beryl was born during the Second World War, in a family that had once been wealthy, but declined over the years. Her father died a few days before the war ended, leaving her mother to raise Beryl, the baby, and her older brother. She was a widow on a tiny pension and no real marketable skills. They went on living in a big house, but it was a draughty old place, it cost a fortune to heat, and they survived on a shoestring.'

Libby, growing up within living memory of the war, had heard many such stories. 'After the war, when education and health improved, did things look up for them?'

'Beryl's mother prided herself on caring her best for Beryl and Cyril. She made a small living with her sewing machine, altering clothes, and the children did well in school. Beryl was a clever girl, especially good at maths. She could have gone to university, but the family was still struggling and Mrs Nightingale persuaded her to get a job, here in Exham, as a secretary. Cyril, of course, being the son, went to university. Exeter, I think, where he gained a respectable degree in law and started to make his way up the ladder as a barrister. Beryl and her mother both doted on Cyril.'

'Beryl stayed quietly at home in Exham, looking after Mrs Nightingale?'

Angela nodded. 'Exactly. But, Beryl had hopes. Cyril's friend, Geoffrey, was also a lawyer, and he and Beryl fell in love. They became engaged and she was all set to marry, set up home in Exeter, and live happily ever after.'

Libby groaned. 'I can sense this isn't going to end happily.'

'You're right. Cyril bought himself a little car. One evening, after a successful case, he and Geoffrey celebrated by driving across the Somerset Levels, visiting public houses. They sped round a corner, straight into a cow that had wandered out from a nearby field. The car pitched into a rhyne, upside down, and both the young men died.'

Libby drew in her breath. 'Those ditches can be treacherous. I've ended up with my front wheels in the water before now.'

'It's easily done, and it was even easier back then, with no lighting in the countryside. The sky was overcast so there was no starlight. No one even found the car until the next morning. Beryl was distraught and Mrs Nightingale was never the same again. They'd both worshipped Cyril, and Beryl truly loved Geoffrey. All her dreams of the future died with him.'

Libby stopped writing, the tragedy of Beryl's loss made more poignant by her own happiness with Max. She made a silent promise never to take her luck for granted. 'That explains the photographs Beryl carried around. The young man must be her old flame. No wonder she kept his picture close. She was left with no qualifications, no fiancé, a dead end job, and a grieving mother.'

'She looked after her mother for years, as Mrs Nightingale

grew more infirm. They became inseparable, with all those shared memories. Beryl never found anyone else to love. She seemed content enough, until her mother died. Mrs Nightingale was well into her eighties, but it came as a dreadful shock to Beryl. She was left all alone in the world. I think that's when the drinking began.'

She fell silent. Libby prompted, 'Come on, you can't stop now.'

'No, I suppose not. The talk in town was that alcohol had always been a problem in the family. I heard Beryl's father was – well – practically an alcoholic as well. Although nothing was certain, the general belief was that Cyril drove the car while he was drunk, and the accident was his fault. People did drink and drive, in those days, before the law changed. There were no breathalysers.' She gave a rueful laugh. 'Folk used to talk about having one more drink before driving. "One for the road," they called it.'

Libby was puzzled. 'I never heard the slightest hint. Not even from Gladys in the flower shop, and she's the biggest gossip in Exham.'

Angela poured more coffee. 'That's the way, around here. We love to gossip, but we're protective of each other when—' She stopped and blushed.

'I know what you mean. When strangers or newcomers are around. Like me.'

Angela's lopsided grin was apologetic. 'There's always been a sort of conspiracy to hide Beryl's problem. Everyone was sorry for her.'

Libby thought back to the society meetings. Beryl had so often offered to give talks about local history, but the talks had never taken place. Other group members always suggested a reason to move on to another topic. Once, Beryl had pulled sheets of lined A4 paper from her bag, but before she could speak, George Edwards had begged for another slice of Libby's cake, to take home to his invalid wife. Margery Halfstead had joined in, praising Libby's baking, and somehow Beryl's talk had been forgotten.

'Are you telling me that when Beryl sat quietly in the corner, waiting to give her lectures, she was sozzled?'

'I'm afraid so. That's why we always found a way to prevent her from starting the talk. I once caught a glimpse of the notes – not even notes, really – merely the stack of paper she kept in her bag.'

Libby nodded. 'Her lecture notes. She used to pull them out and wave them.'

'They made no sense at all; just a few scribbled sentences and a dozen blank pages. Beryl could no more give a talk in public than fly.'

'I had no idea.' Stunned, Libby fell silent. How little she'd understood of Exham's ways. What else did the town gossip hide? 'It's a lot to take in.'

Angela rose and collected cups. 'I think we need more coffee. I suppose we were all – what is it called these days? – enablers. We let Beryl get on with her drinking while we watched out for her, and covered up if she was in danger of embarrassing herself.'

'To save her from strangers like me.' Libby let her breath out in a rush. 'There I was, thinking I'd finally made it into Exham society, but there's so much going on under the surface I don't know about.' She smiled at her friend. 'I won't take it personally. I'm sure any small town's the same.'

While Angela brewed more coffee, Libby thought through the implications of the news. If everyone in the local community knew about Beryl, it would have been easy for her killer to visit on a pretext, and seize a moment when Beryl left the room to slip a dose of poison into a bottle of her favourite tipple.

She followed Angela into the impeccably clean and tidy kitchen. 'Do you know anything about Beryl giving up work? She'd been around town more, recently, popping into the bakery almost every day. Did she just retire, or perhaps she had to leave?'

Angela shrugged. 'Because of the drinking? I didn't hear anything, but some of the others might know. I know she stopped working at the racing stables a few months ago, but she was old enough to retire long ago. She'd worked well beyond retirement age. She'd been with the stables all her life, and I imagine they let her stay on as long as she wanted to. I'm not sure how useful she would have been, in recent years. Another example of mistaken sympathy, perhaps, letting her carry on.'

Angela led the way out of the kitchen. 'We were wrong to ignore her drinking. If we'd been tougher, maybe she could have dealt with the problem, and would still be with us. So much for helping your neighbour. I'm afraid many of us bear a little of the blame for Beryl's sad life.'

Libby remained silent for a long time, thinking, until, seized with a longing to talk it all over with Max, she finished her drink, gathered up her bag, and stood, ready to leave. Angela took her arm on the way out. 'There's something I need to tell you.'

'Not more lurid revelations?'

Angela smiled. 'No, but you won't like it. You remember that smarmy Terence Marchant?'

Libby groaned. 'A while ago he was threatening to start up a rival patisserie in Exham, but he seems to have lost interest, I'm pleased to say.' The look on Angela's face stopped Libby in her tracks. 'Or has he?'

'I heard he's back, and the patisserie will definitely open in a few weeks. He's planning to overwhelm Exham with French pastries, and he's employing a genuine French pastry chef. He thinks you'll be closed down within six months.'

7

CHOCOLATE BISCUIT

Margery Halfstead sat on the chintz covered settee, knitting needles clicking like chattering teeth. From time to time, she glanced over at William, but he seemed engrossed in the televised golf tournament that slowly played itself out in the drizzle of a northern golf course. Margery pressed her lips more tightly together and knitted faster, tugging hard at the wool after every row, obsessively counting stitches.

William had hardly spoken since Beryl Nightingale's death. He'd talked to the police, but refused to discuss anything about the brief interview at the castle, beyond remarking that constables seemed to get younger every year. Margery tried to feel sympathetic. He'd found the body first so he was bound to be upset, but his actions bothered her.

He'd behaved oddly, that day. He'd left the schoolboys alone and she'd had to step in. Then, he hadn't prevented them from seeing the body. There'd been chaos, for a while, with teenagers shouting and screaming. She wouldn't be surprised if there were complaints from parents. Maybe William would lose his position as a guide. That would upset him, she knew. 'Are you all right?' she tried. William just grunted.

Margery went back to her knitting. They'd never been ones for talking about feelings, neither of them. It seemed a bit un-British, really. Even when she'd lost the baby, all those years ago, they hadn't said much. What was there to say? Talking wouldn't change the fact of the miscarriage. In Margery's opinion, people these days were a bit too inclined to throw their private sorrows in everyone else's face.

She stopped knitting. She hadn't thought about that time for months. At first, she'd not been able to forget the baby who never was. He'd been in her thoughts all the time. They'd planned to call him Oscar. Margery was sure he was a boy, though the doctors had never said.

Thrusting a knitting needle into the ball of fawn coloured wool, she decided to finish the sweater later. She didn't feel much like knitting anything today. Her thoughts slid back to those dreadful days, after she came back from the hospital. She supposed William had given away the little jackets she'd knitted for Oscar. He never said, and she never asked where they went.

She zipped up her knitting bag. This was ridiculous. Beryl Nightingale's death was making her maudlin, and sitting in silence wasn't helping. Better to do something. 'Do you want another cup of tea?'

William grunted. 'Not just now.'

Margery heaved herself to her feet and set off towards the kitchen. She'd have one anyway, and a chocolate biscuit to boot.

She looked back. William had pulled his mobile phone from his pocket. He was scrolling through the screen.

Bet he's ringing that Annabel.

The conviction sprang into Margery's head, as if from nowhere, and immediately, she was sure it was true. A noise started up in her ears, like a storm of wind, and for a moment she felt quite dizzy. She steadied herself with one hand on the kitchen table and let her thoughts run free.

She'd been suspicious from the first moment that Annabel woman had come into the room at the castle, all high heels and lipstick. William already knew her, Margery was quite sure, she could tell from the way he grinned at her. He'd fallen over himself to look after her. A hollow, sick sensation took a grip on Margery's insides. The death of Beryl Nightingale hardly seemed to matter compared with William's treachery.

Forgetting to make the tea, Margery staggered back into the sitting room on wobbly legs and opened the knitting bag again. She tried to work but her eyes wouldn't focus.

She drew a long, steadying breath. 'I hope Annabel isn't too upset. Fancy having someone die on your first day. Bet she won't be back at the castle in a hurry.' Talking about the woman was like picking a scab. She knew it was going to hurt, however William answered, but it was impossible to stop.

He glanced up from his phone. 'Sorry? What did you say?'

Playing the innocent.

The sick feeling was turning to anger, boiling inside. She almost shouted, 'I said, what about Annabel.'

'What about her?'

Pretending not to understand, that was his game, was it? 'Tarty little thing.' Margery almost gasped at her own spite.

'I wouldn't say that.'

Under normal circumstances, Margery admired William's ability to keep calm, but today, she wanted a fight. 'I said,' she raised her voice even more, 'I reckon she's no better than she should be.'

William studied her, as if seeing her for the first time, a

puzzled frown on his face. 'I wouldn't know. What makes you say that?'

The doorbell rang. William said, as he always did, 'I wonder who that could be.'

Margery usually replied, 'There's one way to find out,' but instead, forestalling her husband, she jumped up to answer the door herself.

She had her mouth open, ready to say, 'We never do business at the door,' as William always did, but before she could make a sound she stopped, mouth hanging open at the sight of a pair of police officers, a few respectful feet away from the threshold.

The older one, an overweight man of around forty, said, 'Is your husband at home, Mrs Halfstead? My colleague and I would like to talk to him again, if you please.'

The young blonde woman at his side smiled. 'It won't take too long.'

Margery blinked. Of course, the police had said they'd be coming back, but she hadn't expected to see them again so soon. She stepped aside to let them in, just as William appeared from the sitting room. 'You'd better come in.'

* * *

An hour later, the police left. Margery watched as they drove away. She couldn't swallow; her mouth felt like sandpaper. Her hands were shaking. She crossed the room to the settee, but she couldn't sit. She returned to the window, looking down the empty road. The police car was out of sight, now.

She paced from the hall to the kitchen and then back to the sitting room, her head spinning.

What had just happened?

She revisited the scene, trying to make sense of it.

The interview had begun in a friendly way, like a conversation, with the police offering sympathy. 'We know it's a shock to
be involved in a sudden death. We just want to clarify exactly
what happened.'

William told them about the morning in the castle, and the
arrival of Annabel and the schoolboys. Then, Margery
mentioned how William had gone ahead with the boys to the
butler's pantry. The two officers exchanged a glance. 'You were
with the boys, then, Mr Halfstead, while they talked to Miss
Nightingale?'

William glanced at Margery and stammered a little. 'Not
exactly. I had to collect some notes from my car, and I left the
boys to talk. My wife was with them, so they were quite safe, and
there was a script. Young Jason had prepared what he wanted to
say.'

Margery licked dry lips. At the time, she'd been annoyed that
William left her to cope. Beryl's death had overshadowed the incident and she hadn't given it another thought, but now she
wondered why he'd been so keen to leave. That wasn't like him at
all. He was always conscientious, and she'd never known him
leave documents in the car. In fact, she was sure he'd had a file
with him all the time he was in the castle.

What if he'd lied to her, so he could get away on his own?
Why would he do that?

Try as she might to think, she could only imagine two reasons
for William to abandon his charges. Had he left the boys to go
down to the kitchen? Maybe to check something? But, if so, he
would have told her, instead of making up an excuse.

Margery chewed a rough nail, struggling to think straight. If
William had gone to the kitchen, he was there when Beryl died.

Margery shuddered, on the verge of tears. That would mean
he might have – no, she couldn't finish the thought. It scared her.

Surely, he had no reason to harm Beryl Nightingale? She closed her eyes. There must be another reason for his absence.

Yet, to her mind, there could be only one other possibility: that he was with the new volunteer, Annabel. The more she considered his behaviour that morning, the more certain she became.

Now the police had gone, she had to know the truth. She faced William, hands on hips. 'Why did you leave the boys alone? You didn't need to fetch any handouts, did you? Where did you go?'

For the first time in all the years they'd spent together, William looked shifty. Margery could think of no other word for it. He looked away, shuffled his feet and cleared his throat. His glance flickered towards the door, as though he was contemplating escape. Margery put her bulk firmly between her husband and the exit. 'Tell me,' she demanded. 'Right now.'

He coughed. He spluttered. Margery waited until finally, he spoke. 'I went to speak to someone.'

'Someone? Who?'

'It was...'

He'd never been able to lie. Margery poked a finger at his chest. 'You went to see that Annabel, didn't you?'

His face registered surprise – no, horror – and Margery felt sure her suspicions were correct. He licked his lips, then rubbed his chin, as though playing for time before answering. 'I just wanted to check on her. You know, dear, on her first day and all. I thought she'd like to come and meet the boys, maybe talk down the speaking tube as well, or operate the pulley for the serving lift. Get a flavour of the house.'

Margery closed her eyes. 'You went after that – that hussy. I knew it. How long has it been going on?'

'Going on? I-I don't understand.'

'This affair with that woman.' As she spoke, Margery almost believed she could hear their marriage crashing to the ground. All those years together counted for nothing. The shared, never mentioned sorrow at the loss of their baby, the quiet evenings watching TV over a plate of shepherd's pie. It was all a sham.

William was having an affair.

The words seemed to stand out in Margery's brain, like a neon sign. Her husband took a step forward, but she threw out her arms to ward him off. 'Don't you dare come near me, William Halfstead, unless you can deny you went to find that woman – Annabel whatshername.'

The colour drained from his face. 'You've got it wrong. I mean —' He gasped for breath, clutching his hands to his chest. 'I-I...' He lurched forward, mouth open in a soundless scream as he tore at the sweater she'd knitted last Christmas. Eyes fixed on his wife's face, he tottered a few steps, stopped, gave a howl of agony, and dropped to the floor.

Margery screamed.

8

SPAGHETTI CARBONARA

'William Halfstead's in hospital.' Libby put her phone back in her pocket. 'That was Ian Smith. The horrid man's gloating because I can't talk to one of the main suspects. Or at least, not until he recovers from a heart attack, poor chap.' She was in Max's house – so soon to become her own home – eating dinner. They'd hoped to host his son to celebrate his promotion, but Joe and Claire, his wife, had been forced to cancel. The new job had already begun, and Joe was working on a series of armed robberies. 'We'll do dinner for Joe when he has a spare evening,' Libby had said, 'but let's toast his success anyway.'

'Good idea. Any excuse for one of your special feasts. And tonight, we can enjoy a candle lit dinner for two. I'll put on some romantic music. What's on the menu, by the way?'

'An avocado and smoked chicken starter, followed by spaghetti carbonara, and then...'

'Please, say it's bread and butter pudding.'

'Of course it is – but once we're married, I'll have to train you to eat some different desserts. Oh, and Somerset Brie afterwards, if you can manage it.'

'You know your dinners are the only reason I'm marrying you.'

'Actually, you're marrying me because I asked you to.'

'And who am I to disagree?'

Max put the last morsel of spaghetti carbonara in his mouth and moaned with delight. 'No, sorry, it's definitely because of the food. Bring on the pudding.'

'We'd better not eat like this every day. I don't want you keeling over with a stroke, or a heart attack like William Halfstead.'

Max carried the plates out to the kitchen, returning with a dish full of fragrant, spiced pudding, bursting with sultanas, and topped with crisp brown bread slices. 'At least I'd die a happy man.'

'That's not funny. It does happen, you know.'

Max waved the champagne bottle at Libby. 'Let's hope we've both got a few more years in us. Cheers.'

Libby took a deep breath. It was time she told the truth. 'Actually, I've got a confession to make.'

Max replaced the bottle on the table. 'That sounds serious. Should I be worried? What terrible thing have you done in that murky past of yours?'

'I didn't like to say, before, but I don't want to keep secrets, now we're getting married.' She sighed, theatrically. 'The truth is, I really don't like champagne.'

'No! Really? 'Well, who'd have thought it? I guess our marriage will be full of shocks like that.'

He opened a bottle of Australian Pinot Noir for Libby's approval and they returned to William Halfstead's heart attack. 'Do you think he had the attack because he's guilty of killing Beryl and he's feeling remorseful, or because he's innocent and thinks people will blame him anyway?' she asked.

'Or maybe it's neither and he's just unlucky.'

Libby thought about that. 'His wife must be beside herself.'

Max finished the bread and butter pudding. 'Well, as you're officially involved in the investigation, you can question people as much as you like and find out. Just remember what Joe always says. Don't jump to conclusions, just...'

'Follow the evidence. I will. Also, Beryl's not as squeaky clean as we thought.' She told Max about her conversation with Angela.

He frowned. 'Angela's a mine of information. I always knew the Nightingales had their troubles, with the brother's death, but I didn't know them well. I must have left Exham before Beryl's drinking took hold. No one mentioned it when I eventually came back after – well, you know.' Max had only returned to Exham after his daughter died in a riding accident and his marriage broke up. If Joe hadn't followed, complete with job and wife, determined to sort his father out, no one knew what would have happened to Max.

He stood up. 'Shall we finish the wine in my study? It's cosier in there. Come on, Bear.' He looked around, but there was no sign of Bear.

Libby pointed. 'He's usually behind that chair.'

'Was he there earlier? I thought it was quiet this evening, but I put that down to Shipley being away with the trainer. Bear was in the garden this afternoon. We'd better call him in, as it's starting to get dark.'

They stood at the back door, looking out over the garden and fields beyond. Max shouted Bear's name, but nothing happened. No giant dog hurtled up the path. 'That's odd. He never strays.' Max was frowning. 'He must have escaped through the fence.'

'I'm sure he'll be home soon.' Libby tried to sound confident, but she could see Max was unconvinced. Bear was the most faithful and loyal of canine companions, rarely leaving his humans. 'Let's come back out in a quarter of an hour or so, see if he comes home.'

Neither could settle and the last of the wine remained untouched. Together, they filled the dishwasher and tidied the kitchen, each of them frequently, surreptitiously checking their watches.

'Come on,' Libby said at last, and led the way outside. 'Let's give it one more try.'

Finally, hoarse with calling Bear's name, they were forced to admit defeat. Libby squeezed Max's hand. 'I'm sure he'll be back by morning. He must be off on a spree. Maybe he's scented a female and he's hearing the call of the wild.'

'Maybe, though it won't do him any good. The vet's seen to that. I suppose there's nothing we can do tonight,' Max agreed. 'I'll leave the back door open, just in case.'

9

TOAST

Next morning, Bear was still missing. Libby and Max phoned or sent a text to every friend or neighbour they could think of, but no one had seen him. By the middle of the morning, anxious and sad, they had to admit he'd disappeared. 'But, where could he have gone?' Libby wondered aloud. 'I know he can walk for miles, but surely someone would have seen him.' Mechanically, hardly aware of what she was doing, she made coffee and toast.

'I have a really bad feeling about this,' Max confessed. 'But before we panic, let's go back over his whereabouts in the last couple of days.'

'He was with me two days ago,' Libby remembered. 'Then I left him with you while I went over to the castle to drop off the cake.'

'While you were with Angela yesterday, I took him out on the beach. We walked for about eight miles. It's not as though Bear didn't get his exercise. After the walk, I'm sure he fell asleep behind the chair, as usual, and I drove out to buy champagne while you cooked dinner.'

Libby tried to visualise the time she'd spent alone in Max's house, with Bear. 'The doors were open so he could go in and out. I don't remember seeing him at all, really. I was too busy in the kitchen.'

Max screwed up his eyes in concentration. 'I haven't seen or heard him since. He must have wandered off while you cooked.'

'We're not sure that's when he disappeared. He might have followed you when you went out to get the champagne. You usually take him with you.'

'I only popped out for twenty minutes. I thought you'd be watching him.'

Should she have been? Libby felt a little sick. She loved Bear, but it wasn't her fault he'd gone missing. She didn't live here, yet. She defended herself. 'I can't watch him every minute and this is your house.'

'He spends more time with you these days.'

Suddenly annoyed, Libby pushed herself up from the table, spilling half a cup of coffee. Ignoring the mess, she turned her back on Max and made for the door. 'Maybe I look after him better.'

Max said, 'If you took him out more often for proper walks...'

She swung round, an argument on her lips. As she opened her mouth, she suddenly registered the pallor on his face, and the network of worry lines round his eyes. Her harsh words melted away, temper fading as fast as it had appeared. 'Why are we quarrelling?' She returned to the table, pulled a tissue from her pocket, and mopped up the coffee spill.

Max laid his hand on hers. 'Sorry. There's no need for us to argue. It's not your fault.'

She squeezed his fingers. 'Nor yours. We both kept as much of an eye on Bear as we do normally. I expect we're exaggerating things.'

'Pre-wedding nerves?' Max threw his arms round her, giving one of the hugs she loved.

'I can't understand it.' She nestled into his arms. 'He's never escaped from the garden before. I hope nothing's happened to him, that's all.' Max walked to the window. He peered through the glass, arms folded, miles away, deep in thought.

'Wait a minute.' He left the room at a run. Libby waited patiently. He'd had one of his ideas, and he'd tell her what it was, soon enough. He returned, clutching a glossy magazine full of Somerset news, pictures of impossibly elegant, stately home gardens, and advertisements for houses that no one she knew could afford. 'I'm sure I saw an article...'

Flipping through the pages, he stopped near the end and turned the magazine until Libby could read it.

MISSING PETS

Seven Somerset residents have reported the loss of family pets in the past month. Mrs Johnson of Williton told our reporter her shi-tzu went missing from her garden two days ago. 'He's been with us for years. Of course, he's a pedigree animal, registered with the Kennel Club, so he's worth a lot of money in the market. But we keep him as a family pet, and my two children are devastated.

Martin Anderson, a farmer in West Somerset, reported his Border collie stolen, two weeks ago. The animal, a working sheepdog, lived in a specially built kennel near the house. 'They must have drugged him,' Mr Anderson insisted. 'He'd never go willingly with anyone. He's a highly trained, tremendously valuable dog who's won prizes in television's One Man and his Dog.'

Max's eyes met Libby's. 'It looks as though someone's stealing valuable animals.'

A painful lump took up residence in Libby's throat. If Bear

had been stolen, he might be gone for good. He'd become almost as important to her as Max and her children. He'd been with her on all her adventures. In fact, it was the dog who first introduced her to Max. Idiotically, she said, 'What will Fuzzy do without him?' After an initial spat, the marmalade cat had become firm friends with the giant dog.

Max heaved a sigh. 'Well, we're supposed to be private investigators. It looks as though we'll have to do some investigation on our own behalf, this time. The bitcoin fraud will have to wait. I'll start with Google, if you'll speak to your friend, Tanya the vet. Maybe she knows about this.' Tanya had once nursed Fuzzy's broken leg, and was one of Bear's devoted friends.

'Has Bear been chipped?' Libby asked. 'I never thought to ask.'

'Yes, I had it done when old Mrs Thomson died and I adopted him.'

Libby slipped on a waxed jacket. 'I'll print out some poster-sized pictures of Bear and visit Tanya now to find out what she knows, but then I have to spend the rest of the morning in the bakery. I promised Frank I'd work this shift with Mandy while he does some special deliveries on the other side of town. Oh!'

'What is it?'

'I'll have to tell Mandy. She'll be devastated.'

* * *

The vet was full of sympathy as Libby showed her the magazine article. She knew Bear well. 'I've heard about this; several animals have disappeared, and the thieves seem likely to be professionals, if they're able to whisk huge animals like Bear out of sight.' She nodded. 'The victims are mostly valuable dogs, so the police have been involved. Have you talked to Joe?'

Libby clicked her tongue in annoyance. 'Do you know, I never thought of that. Are the police taking it seriously?'

Tanya shrugged. 'They came to see me, but I couldn't help. They sent Constable Ian Smith, though, and I can't imagine he'll put himself out too much over missing animals.' Her expression made it plain PC Smith was no more popular with her than with Libby. 'He loves to catch children riding their bikes on the pavement on the way to school, but he's too lazy to go out of his way to offer a helping hand.'

The vet sighed, 'I miss the old days of policemen on bikes. We have a pair of community police officers who call in from time to time, and they're more sympathetic than PC Smith, but it's not the same.' She laughed. 'I'm showing my age. Anyway, I reckon the police have more important things to worry about. Like this business up at the castle.' She looked at Libby, a question on her face. She was always in the market for gossip.

Libby hesitated. She had to be careful not to give away unauthorised information. Sometimes it was harder working with the police than independently. Still, there seemed no harm in telling Tanya the bare bones of the story, leaving out any information that could identify the schoolchildren involved. Tanya had helped her out before, with information leading to the exposure of the Glastonbury Tor killer, who'd recently begun a sentence of fifteen years in HM Prison Exeter.

After some thought, she even told Tanya about William's heart attack. He was a well-known figure in the area, one of the members of the recently reformed Exham on Sea History Society, and a popular guide at the castle. The vet might be able to throw some light on the man and his wife.

Tanya made a sympathetic face. 'I've been on a tour of the servants' quarters with him at Dunster Castle,' she said. 'He's a charming man, although his wife can be difficult. They used to bring their Highland terrier here, but sadly, he passed away a few months ago. I don't think William and Margery have got over it. That dog was like a child to them.'

That gave Libby an idea. She wanted to talk to Margery about the death at Dunster Castle, but she needed an excuse to visit. Now she had one; if she was a dog lover, she'd be sympathetic about Bear. She'd probably be willing to put up a poster in her window.

The idea wasn't brilliant, but the best Libby could dredge up for the moment. In any case, she wouldn't be visiting until tomorrow. It was past time for her to start work in the bakery, and she refused to let Frank down.

Tanya made a suggestion. 'Why don't we organise a proper search for Bear?'

'We're planning to put up posters on lampposts and so on. That was how I found Mrs Marchant's missing cat.' Libby felt a familiar twinge of anxiety, for Mrs Marchant's son was the same Terence Marchant who seemed determined to put Brown's Bakery out of business.

She didn't have time to think about Terence Marchant today. She was too worried about Bear. 'Here's one of the posters. Would you put it up in your waiting room?' The sight of Bear's face, so big and gentle, with enormous, soulful brown eyes, almost broke her heart.

Tanya took the poster. 'Of course, and I'll ring round other dog owners on the books. You know they'll all be willing to turn out and search. It makes walking the dog more interesting than usual, and the weather's respectable today. In any case, plenty of my clients know Bear, and everyone loves him. I'm not too busy today, apart from the surgery.'

She waved in the general direction of the waiting area, which was filling fast with an assortment of over-excited, yappy young dogs, grumpy cats in baskets, clearly wishing they could escape and see off the puppies, and a couple of sickly looking hamsters.

By the time Libby made her way to the door, through the throng of sympathetic pet owners, she was horribly late for work, but at least five people had promised to get out into the fields and woodland around Exham and join the search. If Bear was anywhere near Exham on Sea, Libby was confident he'd soon be found.

10

BREAD

Mandy was busy tweaking the display of Mrs Forest's Chocolates in the bakery window. Despite her wild black hair, which was styled today in a series of spikes, the slash of purple lipstick across her mouth, and her status as Exham's resident Goth, she was a popular member of the Brown's Bakery team. Even Frank, the proprietor, had grown used to her weird appearance.

She greeted Libby's arrival with a sympathetic hug and a barrage of questions. 'I couldn't believe it when I got your text. Did Bear just wander off? Have you made posters? Will you be able to get him back, d'you think?'

'I'll find him, or die trying.' Libby explained the situation to Frank. 'I'm so sorry to be late,' she finished.

'Don't you worry. Mandy and I have been managing just fine.' He hesitated. 'Since you arrived in town, Libby, with your cakes and chocolates, the turnover in this place has trebled. If there's anything I can do to help, just let me know.'

Libby had to blow her nose, suddenly overcome with emotion. Frank never wasted words, and he avoided emotion like the plague.

As Libby attached posters to every spare space, inside and outside the shop, Frank pulled loaves from the kitchen oven, visibly relieved to get back to business. 'That's the lot for today.' He peeled off his gloves. 'If you're ready to take over, I'll leave you two alone this morning while I make my rounds. I'll tell everyone I meet about Bear, and don't you worry about that animal. He can look after himself.'

Mandy nodded vigorously. 'Of course, he can. He probably got himself stuck in an outhouse overnight. He'll give someone a fright when they open the door.'

Frank untied his apron. 'Those new chocolates are selling brilliantly.'

'Well, I can't take the credit,' Libby confessed, determined to be business-like. 'They were Mandy's idea. I'd never have thought of treacle tart flavoured filling.'

Mandy, blushing through her makeup, stacked loaves of bread on the shelves to hide her face, just as the bell rang to herald the daily flood of lunchtime customers.

'Here we go,' said Frank. 'I'm off.' He hated chatting to customers. He'd find any excuse to leave the bakery during the rush for sandwiches.

Libby welcomed the sudden influx of business. Maybe it would take her mind off Bear.

Every customer had plenty to say. Even if they weren't dog people, there was a lot to discuss: Bear's disappearance, the death at the castle, and William Halfstead's heart attack were all hot topics.

'It's a funny thing,' Libby murmured, passing Mandy on the trail of pizza slices for a group of hungry teenagers. 'Have you noticed how we double our customer numbers when there's something for them to gossip about?'

Before long, Gladys from the flower shop arrived and pointed at Bear's poster. Libby's heart missed a beat, as it did every time she looked at the dog's face beaming down from the wall. 'That's why I would never have a pet. It's too easy to get fond of them.'

Mandy muttered to Libby, 'I can't imagine that woman being fond of anyone or anything.' Libby suspected the reason she came into the bakery was to pick up on the day's news, so that she could pass it on, with embellishments, to her own customers.

Libby whispered, 'In her defence, she's good at her job. She sold me a beautiful autumn bouquet of dahlias – or, were they chrysanthemums, I never know the difference – last week.'

Mandy scoffed. 'Aren't chrysanthemums the flowers people put on graves?'

Libby paused, disconcerted, a half-wrapped cob loaf in her hands. 'Are they? I didn't know that.'

'They are in Belgium, anyway. We had a school trip there, to see the battlefield at Ypres, and they told us. It's bad luck to give them as a gift.'

'Really? Oh dear, I gave them to the new doctor's wife a while ago, when she invited me to tea. Don't laugh. I've had an idea, though.' She raised her voice. 'Could you make me up a rather special bouquet of flowers for Margery Halfstead? I want to visit her later today. But no chrysanthemums, thanks.'

'How about Michaelmas daisies and Chinese lanterns?'

'Perfect. I'll pick them up this afternoon.'

Gladys had a theory about William's heart attack. 'It's the cholesterol,' she said, taking possession of two pastries in a paper bag.

Libby avoided Mandy's eye, for fear of bursting into laughter. Gladys clearly didn't see the irony in her high cholesterol purchase. 'But I hear the heart attack happened just after a visit from the police.'

The woman's eyes flittered between her listeners. 'Those

police officers may have a case to answer, if I'm not mistaken. Harassment, you know.'

James, the newsagent, hurrying to collect his lunchtime sandwiches, paused a moment to add his thoughts before rushing from the shop. 'Annabel Pearson was up at the castle when Beryl Nightingale died. She told my wife Mr Halfstead looked fine at the time.'

Libby listened to the gossip without contributing. The bakery often produced useful titbits. When she talked to customers outside the shop, they remembered her job as a private investigator and grew tight-lipped, but inside the shop, they seemed to regard her as part of the furniture.

Gladys showed no sign of leaving. 'I can't imagine why anyone would want to kill Beryl Nightingale. She never did any harm in her life, though she didn't do much of anything, come to think of it.'

Mandy rolled her eyes at Libby. It seemed Gladys was perfectly happy to speak ill of the dead.

At least she didn't appear to know about Beryl's secret drink problem.

A couple of cashiers from the bank juggled sandwiches, cakes, and bottles of pop to take back to their colleagues. Marianne, the youngest, a girl of around Mandy's age wearing an impossibly tight skirt, her hair scraped into a ponytail on top of her head, said, 'Beryl was a sort of relative of my mother. She used to do the books for the racing stables until she retired.'

'Retired? Is that what she called it?' Her colleague, Adrian Waller, an older man wearing horn-rimmed spectacles and a baggy blue suit, snorted.

Gladys turned at the hint of gossip. 'Go on. You can't stop there. It sounds as though there's a story to be had.'

Adrian Waller was already in full flow. 'There was a discrepancy. In the books. That's what I heard.'

Gladys gasped, her eyes glittering with excitement. 'No. Really? Who would have thought it?'

Marianne looked close to tears. 'I don't know where that story came from, but Aunt Beryl was as honest as the day is long, so there.' She elbowed the door of the shop and left, slamming the door in her colleague's face. He grimaced and followed meekly behind.

'He'll be wishing he kept his mouth shut,' another customer observed.

The bakery fell silent, and Gladys took her leave. 'I'm sure none of us meant any harm.' She hesitated at the door. 'I'll make up that bouquet for you right away, Libby. I'll make it special. No one can say I don't do my bit in the community.'

At last, the shop was empty. 'Well.' Mandy let her breath out in a sigh. 'That was interesting. Will you be investigating Beryl Nightingale's death, Mrs F, or are you too busy looking for Bear?'

Libby, scribbling in her notebook, hardly heard. Mandy shook her head. 'If only you'd learn to make notes on your phone, you'd save yourself, like, hours of work.'

11

LAYER CAKE

While Libby had spent the second half of the morning at the bakery, Max had abandoned his computer in favour of the search for Bear, co-ordinating with the vet's band of volunteers. He returned cold, wet, and dirty, but with no good news. 'If Bear's anywhere between here and Taunton, we'd have found him.'

He looked as despondent as Libby felt. She fed him coffee while he listed the places the helpers had searched and told her about a call he'd had from Joe, 'He filled me in on the reported animal thefts in the area. The cases are still open, but he says the police don't have enough manpower to prioritise them. We'll have to find Bear ourselves.'

He took another mouthful of coffee. 'That's better. How about a slice of toast? Or, even better, coffee cake?'

As Libby cut a hefty slice, calculating that hours in the countryside had earned Max a decent reward, he talked with renewed enthusiasm. 'I've tracked down a string of similar disappearances across the south-west, mostly valuable animals. No ransom demands, so far. That's good, I think, because it means the animals must be of use to the thieves.' That was something to hold onto.

'Several are trained sheepdogs, like Bear,' he pointed out. 'Would they have some sort of market value as working animals? No one's tried to take Shipley, even though he's a much better sniffer dog. He's only got another day or two with the trainer, by the way. He'll miss his canine mate.'

'Don't write Bear off like that,' Libby pleaded. 'We'll get him back. We just need to work a bit harder.'

'I'm doing all I can.'

'I know.' Libby tried to smile. She was taking her feelings out on Max again, although she knew it wasn't his fault. 'Sorry.' She kissed his cheek.

Max enveloped her in his arms. 'We're both upset, but we're professional investigators. We'll find him. You follow up on Beryl's case, and I'll keep tracking down other missing animals. There must be common links, and if there are, I shall find them. They don't call me Meticulous Max for nothing.'

Reluctantly, Libby laughed. 'I've never heard anyone call you that.'

'No. I made it up. Now, you're looking more cheerful. Go and find out more about William Halfstead.'

Libby was eager to visit Margery Halfstead, to find out the truth about William's heart attack. She stopped on the way to pick up her flowers. They were beautiful. Gladys surprised Libby. 'I'm giving you a 50 per cent discount.'

'That's far too generous.'

Gladys blew her nose. 'I think I was a little harsh this morning. I'm sorry about William, and Beryl too, of course. Give Margery my regards.'

She travelled through a maze of small streets on the modern housing estate where Margery and William Halfstead lived, trying not to think of Bear. He should have been in the back of her cramped Citroen, slobbering on her seat. Instead, he was missing.

Margery Halfstead answered the door wearing an apron and carrying a duster. For a moment, Libby wondered if her husband had come home from hospital, and things were back to normal in the Halfstead household. Then, she remembered her own mother's habit of undertaking vigorous housework at times of stress. Libby used baking in the same way. She'd spent the previous evening constructing an elaborate layer cake that neither she nor Max would ever eat.

Margery peered out suspiciously. 'Are you from the police?'

'I'm Libby Forest. I work with the police, but I'm not a proper officer. I mean, I don't arrest people, or anything.'

The fierce lines on Margery's face relaxed. 'In that case, you can come in. I won't have the police in my house, not after what happened to my husband.'

'I heard. We're all very sorry, in the history society, and other people too. Here, these are from me and – er – the lady in the flower shop.'

'Gladys? Oh, yes, we've known her for years. Come in.'

Libby followed her into the house, and Margery took the flowers out to the kitchen while Libby sat on a fifties style G Plan sofa, watching coloured blobs of lava rising and falling in a nearby lamp. When Margery returned, holding a tall jug in which she'd arranged the flowers, she nodded towards the lamp. 'That was a wedding present. It's still working, after all these years.'

Libby made approving noises. 'You've been married a long time, Mrs Halfstead.'

'Call me Margery. Yes, and never a cross word.'

'Really?' Libby blinked. She and Max argued endlessly. The truth was, she rather enjoyed their sparring bouts, and they always led to a happy reconciliation. What must it be like never to disagree?

Tears glistened in Margery's eyes. 'Not until the other day, that is. I – I was angry with him.' She took a shuddering breath. 'It's all my fault he's so ill. It wasn't the police that made him ill. It was me.' She burst out crying, sobbing with such heartbreak that Libby had no idea how to help. Instead, she sat in impotent silence, waiting for the storm of grief to pass.

Margery blew her nose. 'I'm sorry. Look at me, I must be a mess.'

'No, not at all. Of course, you're upset and worried. You've a right to a few tears.' Libby longed to know the cause of the quarrel, but hardly knew how to ask.

Luckily, Margery wanted to talk. 'I was stupid, and – and jealous. I said some dreadful things. I accused him. I accused William of having an affair. As if he would.'

Libby stole a glance at the black and white wedding photograph on top of the old-fashioned television. Even on his wedding day, William Halfstead did not look like the kind of man to have affairs. He was neither handsome nor dashing. A touch overweight, with a gigantic nose and long ears, thinning hair, and crooked teeth, he gazed with devotion down at his short, plain bride. Still, it was not looks that mattered. Perhaps William had a dashing personality.

'An affair?' she prompted.

'Yes, with that hussy – Annabel thing.'

Annabel Pearson was half William's age. Surely, his wife was imagining things. Was that what happened when you'd been married for years? It wasn't going to spoil things with Max – Libby caught herself up. Hadn't she been ridiculously jealous of Kate Stephenson, the 'alternative therapist' he'd spent time with recently? And hadn't his interest been just a matter of furthering their investigation? Surely Margery Halfstead was allowed to be as foolish as Libby.

Margery was talking about the day of Beryl's death. 'There were several volunteers there, that morning, getting on with the annual clean. I didn't recognise all of them, because Mrs Moffat had taken on new people. Annabel was there for the first time and William went off after her when he was supposed to be looking after the schoolboys.' Her hand flew to her mouth, as though she wanted to take back her words.

She glared at Libby, fierce as a tiger protecting her cubs. 'Now, don't you go telling people that. It was only a second or two he was away from them, and they were safe with me. I don't want him to lose his job.'

Libby said nothing. If William had been responsible for Beryl's death, whether deliberately or not, losing an unpaid volunteer position at the castle would be the least of his worries.

'Anyway.' Margery sniffed. 'I'd gone upstairs to set off one of the bells the family used to call their servants. The boys would hear it jangling, down in the servants' quarters. There was another woman upstairs, one of the other volunteers. I don't know her name. My head's a bit woolly. Anyway, I was on the verge of telling her about the bell when we heard a scream. Ooh, such a dreadful noise. It gave me the shivers. I ran down the stairs and into the Victorian kitchen, and there was Beryl on the floor.'

She dusted a porcelain figure, one of a pair. A shepherd and shepherdess, so far as Libby could see. She asked, 'That volunteer you saw at the castle. Can you remember more about her?'

Margery paused. 'I've seen her before, once or twice, but she's not friendly. Shy, I suppose. I like to live and let live. Funny clothes, the ones she wears. Bright, you know, and summer frocks even at this time of year. Too much makeup, I've noticed, but her hair's nice. Black and glossy.'

'You don't know her name?'

'We were never introduced. Funny, though, she reminded me of someone...'

Libby waited, but Margery shook her head. 'No, I can't think.'

Libby stood. 'I hope your husband gets well soon.'

Margery had regained some composure. 'At least the doctors say he's only had a mild heart attack – more a bit of angina, they said – and he can come home tomorrow.'

'And you can make up your quarrel.'

Margery peered round the room. 'I need to make the place spick and span for him.'

Libby took the hint, handed Margery a business card, and left. She hadn't even had to use Bear's posters as an excuse.

Margery closed the door behind her guest, sought out a pot of Brasso, and began work on the door handles, buffing them to a brilliant shine. She'd always said, a clean home is a happy home.

As she worked, pictures of that day at the castle ran through her brain, like watching a film. They'd been working together so happily, William following her lead in the cleaning, waiting until it was time to look after the students. She smiled, remembering the frown on his face as he'd tried to copy her practised flick of the wrist when dusting ancient books.

Then that woman had arrived. Margery's hand froze in mid-polish. She could still hear the heels clacking on the floor, and smell the woman's flowery perfume. Annabel. Annabel who? What was the woman's last name? Had she even told them? And why would a woman like her, young, pretty – even Margery had to admit she looked good – turn up to volunteer in a stately home. Had she come specifically to see William, or was there some other attraction?

Margery sat down. She needed to be comfortable to think. Who else had been in the castle that day? There were the other members of the history society, of course, and a volunteer or two unknown to Margery. Beryl, William and herself, Annabel, and Angela had popped in for half an hour. Libby had not been there until later, with the cake. There were the paid staff, including Mrs Moffat. Then the students had arrived for their visit.

There was nothing unusual about any of it, except that the castle should have been closed for cleaning. For some reason, it had been reopened for Jason Franklin and the other students. Was that because he was an MP's son? Margery hadn't given the matter much thought. She vaguely remembered William talking on the phone, arranging the schoolboys' visit.

A nasty suspicion entered her head. Could it have been Annabel on the other end of the call? And if so, why had she and William wanted the schoolboys in the castle that day?

Margery looked down at her hands. They were trembling. A terrible fear had closed its grip. Was Beryl's death part of a plan, something diabolical Margery did not yet understand? Had the unfortunate woman stumbled upon a secret, and died as a result? And, if that was so, could it possibly be – no, she wouldn't even think it. William would never...

Margery could sit there no longer. She had to find out. She couldn't ask her husband outright, even when he recovered. She was sure of nothing, and nobody, any more. She would have trusted William with her life, but what if he'd been pulling the wool over her eyes for years over an affair with Annabel? What if it had led to a plot involving schoolboys and MPs' sons, uncovered by silly, innocent Beryl who'd had to die as a result?

It was all too much for Margery to deal with on her own. Her head was spinning. She rested it in her hands, the thoughts whirring round, too dreadful to contemplate. She needed help in working things out.

Shakily, she took out the piece of card from her apron pocket.

She dialled the number and heard it ring on the other end. There was a click. 'Hello,' said a voice. Before Margery could answer, her own doorbell rang. 'One minute,' she said into the phone, laid it carefully on its side, making sure not to scratch the polished table, and hurried to the front door.

The visitor wore a big coat and a headscarf. Margery peered at her. 'Can I help—'

She hardly saw the metallic flash of the knife before it plunged into her body, just below the pocket of her apron.

She staggered back, clutching her side, where blood already seeped through her clothes. Her mouth stretched wide as she made a sound between a scream and a gasp, before she tumbled through the door into the sitting room.

As the world turned dark, the last thing she heard was a tinny voice from the phone calling, 'Hello? Who's there? Is everything all right?'

12

ASPIRIN

The phone line was still open. Libby listened with growing horror as she heard the grating, gasping cry, followed by a crash, and sudden silence. 'Hello,' she called again. 'What's going on?' But there was only the empty sound of a telephone line.

'Max,' she shouted. 'Come here.' He came running, and she pointed to the receiver. There's someone on the other end, and – well – I think they've collapsed, or died, or—'

Max took the phone from her hands, listened a moment, then pulled out his mobile. 'We'd better keep the line open while we get help. Who's on the other end?'

'I don't know. They didn't say a word. I just answered the phone and there were all these noises. Ooh, Max, it was horrible. Like someone dying. We have to get help.'

He was already talking on his mobile. 'Right, let me know.'

He clicked off the phone. 'The police will trace the call. Good job you kept the line open. I wonder why they were ringing on the landline. Hardly anyone uses that, these days.'

Libby cried out. 'Oh, Max. I gave the number to Margery Halfstead when I left. I think she's been taken ill.'

'Let's get over there.'

In moments, they were in the Land Rover, speeding through the lanes, but at Margery and William's neat little house on the estate, they found the police had arrived first, along with an ambulance. The paramedics bundled someone into the ambulance, but Libby couldn't tell if the patient was alive or dead.

'Max, if she's dead, it will be my fault. She was contacting me to tell me something vital, I'm sure. I should never have visited her.' The words flew from her lips in a jumbled stream, hardly making sense even to Libby.

'Let's not panic until we have to,' Max advised, gripping her hand. His fingers were large and warm, and Libby clung on as though her own life depended on keeping him close.

PC Ian Smith came over. 'Thought I recognised the car. You again, Mrs Forest?'

Libby was too distraught to care that it was PC Smith. 'Is she OK?'

'She's still alive, at least.'

'Oh, thank heaven.' Relief rushed over Libby's body.

'She's not at all well, though. She's been stabbed.'

Libby gasped. 'She was on the phone. She rang me.'

Smith's habitual expression of faint disbelief changed to excitement. 'You mean, you heard what happened?'

Within seconds, he'd bundled Libby into the back of the police car to give her statement. As she finished the story, he snapped his notebook shut. 'You can go, now. We'll get back to you.' He gave a short bark of a laugh. 'You know the procedure, by now.'

* * *

'Maybe you should take the rest of the afternoon off.' Max was feeding Libby tea and biscuits.

'I'm quite all right,' she insisted, and grimaced. She sounded tetchy. A dose of aspirin had failed to cure the pounding in her head. 'I shall go home and feed Fuzzy. I've been neglecting her, recently, and she'll be missing Bear, too. I'll feel better if I'm doing something.'

'If that's what you want, I'll come with you.'

Tempted, for she felt calmer in Max's presence, Libby made herself turn down the offer. 'We need to push on. There's so much to do. I promised the police I'd talk to the other members of the history society. They'll be horrified; William and Margery are both founder members. I'm sure they'll know a lot more about Beryl, especially her – er – private life.'

'You mean, the secret drinking?'

'Exactly.'

'Good idea. Meanwhile, I'll go and visit Shipley with his new trainer, and track down some of the other people who've lost dogs. They may know what's going on.'

'Shipley. Do you know, I'd forgotten? He should be a fully paid-up sniffer dog by now.'

'He'll never reach the heights of expertise of some of the police dogs. His training came too late. An old dog, you know, and new tricks.'

'Nonsense. Shipley's very talented, and still young. He just needs a little direction. He'll be a star, working with the police. Oh.' She sat up straight, struck by the obvious. 'Maybe we could use him. Not just to find Bear, but in the business.'

'It's a thought. Meanwhile, I'm sure he can help lead us to Bear, if only we knew where to look. If anyone will know Bear's scent, it's Shipley.'

13

CHOCOLATE CAKE

Libby was keen to get to the history society meeting the next day, at George Edward's house. It would help take her mind off Bear. Besides, the attack on Margery, while Libby was listening, had shaken her to the core, and the members of the society must know more about Beryl than anyone else in Exham. The society had been a huge part of her life.

The prospect of meeting George's wife, Deirdre, piqued Libby's curiosity. The woman was surrounded by an air of mystery, for she rarely attended meetings. Ill health prevented her from getting out much, but Libby had only the vaguest idea of her illness. One of those 'female things' George's generation was reluctant to talk about. George often left meetings early, to look after Deirdre. He'd developed a habit of claiming the final portion of cake, supposedly for his wife.

Libby, the main contributor of that cake, had brought a crunchy, chocolate affair today. It was designed to cheer any members distressed by Beryl's death, William's illness, and the attack on Margery. Libby found chocolate was a great cure for mild depression.

The small group huddled in the Edwards' home seemed diminished, not only in number, but also in spirits. There were two new members: Joanna, the young wife of the newly arrived local doctor, who was also the recipient of Libby's flowers, and Annabel Pearson. As Libby arrived, Joanna was moving from one member to another, flirting with the men and telling the women about the latest escapades of her two children. She took a substantial slice of cake and gushed, 'Mrs Forest, how lovely to see you again. I've heard so much about your baking. In fact, my husband insists I call in to the bakery at least once a week. He's determined to sample your whole product range, one cake at a time.'

Mrs Moffat, the castle housekeeper, not required at the castle., was also there. Even the winter cleaning had been suspended for a few days following Beryl's death, while police enquiries continued, and the housekeeper was enjoying her freedom. 'Joanna's been showing me photographs of her delightful children,' she enthused. 'Mine are grown up, now, and would you believe I miss their noise and mess? My house is far too tidy, these days.'

She turned to Annabel, who sat quietly on an uncomfortable looking chair. 'You have children, too, I believe?'

'Just one. James.' Annabel bit her lip, as though unwilling to chat.

Mrs Moffat tried again. 'I wanted to thank you for helping out at the castle. It's so nice to have younger people involved. Most of us are a little "over the hill".'

Annabel nodded in silence, and Mrs Moffat, clearly tired of making the effort to be friendly with so little reward, resumed her livelier conversation with Joanna, gossiping excitedly under their breath about Beryl's death and William Halfstead's heart attack.

Libby circled the room, serving cake. It was a useful way to observe people without becoming embroiled in conversation.

From time to time, Joanna glanced her way. Checking what kind of impression she's making? A bit too eager to please for Libby's liking.

Annabel looked depressed. Libby, aware that William's heart attack had followed a quarrel with his wife, and knowing Annabel was the cause of the argument, used a general conversational hum as camouflage to murmur, 'I'm so sorry about what happened at the castle, on your first day.'

Annabel gave a tired smile, as though making a special attempt. 'Thank you. It was a shock.'

'And then, poor William's heart attack.' Libby made a pretence of struggling to balance the cake plate on a miniscule table, measuring the younger woman's reaction through half closed eyes.

Annabel gulped. 'He was very kind to me on my first day. A lovely man, I thought.'

What did her wide-eyed expression mean? Simple distress, sadness that a good man was gravely ill, or evidence of a closer, clandestine relationship?

Libby moved on, listening to the small talk in the room. Joanna seemed determined to admire everything and everyone. 'I love this room,' she gushed. A print on the wall caught her eye. 'Is that Dunkery Beacon?'

'By a local artist. We have almost as many painters in Somerset as in St Ives.'

'And those trophies?' Joanna had moved on to a group of three silver cups in a sideboard.

'Oh, those.' George moved in front of the cabinet, blocking Libby's view. 'Just a few fishing trophies. I belong to the Exham on Sea club. When we're not sea fishing, we go over to Wimbleball Lake.'

George's wife, Deirdre, raised her voice for the first time.

'George is one of the club's champions. Always winning prizes. Some of the local landowners are members of the club, you know. And I believe our MP takes part, from time to time. He was there, that time someone accused you of cheating. So unfair! As if you would do such a thing.'

George fidgeted, shifting from one foot to the other. 'No one wants to know about the fishing today, dear.' He took his wife's hand, solicitous. 'Are you quite comfortable there? Not in a draught?'

'Dear George,' his wife murmured. 'Always so considerate.'

Deirdre Edwards intrigued Libby. Lying back in the largest armchair in the room, she wore an all-enveloping dress in a vibrant floral material, including, it seemed, every colour shade in an artist's armoury. Her head leaned back against the chair, as though she lacked sufficient strength to keep it upright.

George sat close, handing her teacup to her whenever she needed a sip, constantly checking whether she was too hot, or a little chilly so near the window, whether she would be more comfortable on the sofa, or if she was tired and needed to rest.

To each of his inquiries, Deirdre replied with a gentle smile and a murmured, 'I feel quite well, at present. I can manage a few more minutes, I think.' Her eyes belied her languid pose. An unusual shade of blue green that appeared to change colour according to the light, they flickered tirelessly from one speaker to another, watching. She was an attractive woman. Her black hair, perhaps an unusually bright black for a woman of her age, was beautifully styled and curled gently round her face.

George patted his wife's hand and stood, addressing the group members with unusual authority. 'Thank you all for coming today. It seemed right to meet, in honour of our dear friend, Beryl, who passed away so sadly. Some society members were present at the castle that morning,' he nodded to Mrs Moffat, the housekeeper, 'and were privileged to be the last to speak to Beryl. My wife, Deirdre, has been a long-time friend to Beryl, and she suggested a memorial.'

Deirdre raised a hand in acknowledgement. 'Beryl was such a support when I returned home from hospital. She used to arrive every week with a big container of beef stew.'

Libby wished she'd taken the time to discover what had been wrong with George's wife. She'd assumed her poor health had been just an excuse, used to avoid social events she preferred not to attend.

She offered another slice of cake. Deirdre shook her head. Her hair stayed oddly still, in the same neat style, and Libby realised it must be a wig. How could she not have noticed before? She'd thought Deirdre dyed her hair, the colour a little dark for her pale complexion, but then, who didn't? The poor woman must have been having treatment, probably for cancer. And you call yourself an investigator?

Joanna said, 'I think it's wonderful that you've all gathered here today. I only met Miss Nightingale once, but I found her completely charming.'

Libby fought back an inappropriate smile. Charming was one of the last words she would have chosen to describe mousy little Beryl, even before Angela's revelations.

George continued. 'We must also acknowledge the dreadful tragedies that have fallen on our friends, Margery and William Halfstead. I can hardly believe what happened.' His weather-beaten face fell into such a desolate expression that Libby feared he was about to cry. Instead, he turned to her. 'I'm pleased we have Libby Forest with us, not just for the cake, of course.' He gave a short laugh, but no one joined in, and he cleared his throat before continuing. 'In her role as a private detective, she may know more about the events of the past few days.'

Caught unawares, Libby was forced to point out she could not divulge any information from the police. 'Really,' she confessed, 'I'm here to find out more about Beryl and Margery, as I suppose there's a high probability whoever killed Beryl was responsible for the attack on Margery.'

Her words unleashed a torrent of anger, sympathy, and horror, as the group members debated, with great vigour and animation, in the absence of any factual information, what could have led to the attacks.

'Beryl never hurt a fly,' George stated. 'At least, not when she was herself.'

George's wife, Deirdre, roused herself enough to remark, 'Actually, I found her a little strange.' A hush fell on the room as though a silent agreement had been broken. For a moment, the stillness lasted, until, liberated from politeness now the words were out and the conspiracy broken, the group began to tell the truth.

'She could be difficult, sometimes, especially if she was, well, under the weather,' George said.

'She wasn't always the best time keeper,' Mrs Moffat added. 'She was often late arriving for her shifts at the castle, and once or twice, she seemed just a little...' She swallowed. 'A little unwell. But her heart was in the right place.'

George gave a short laugh. 'Unwell, indeed! It was the demon drink that got Beryl. She could be spiteful when she had a tipple. It loosens the tongue a bit too much for my liking.'

His wife put a hand on his arm. 'Poor Beryl,' she said.

George patted his wife's hand and shook his head sanctimoniously. 'Yes indeed. Sad, very sad. Good thing she had friends to look out for her.'

His words acted as a brake on the group's chatter. They fell to a discussion of a suitable memorial. A collection, they agreed, would be appropriate, spent on an appropriate reminder of Beryl. 'Perhaps a bench in the seafront gardens?' Joanna ventured.

George announced he would make a visit to the hospital with Mrs Moffat, to take chocolates to Margery and William as soon as they were well enough, and the meeting seemed about to break up in a spirit of agreement when Joanna, her clear voice rising above the chatter, said, 'Of course, when we arrived in Exham, we were told about that unfortunate business with Miss Nightingale and the accounts.'

A hush fell, and all heads turned. Libby ventured, 'Accounts?'

Joanna glanced from one to the other, eyes very blue. 'Oh dear, have I spoken out of turn? I thought it was common knowledge that poor Miss Nightingale was asked to leave the racing stables she worked for. A matter of finance, you know. So sorry. Perhaps I'm mistaken.' The half smile on her lips belied her words.

Libby narrowed her eyes. That one knows exactly what she's doing. Did that make her a suspect, or just spiteful?

'I'm sure it was a misunderstanding,' George said. 'She told me she wanted to retire, to spend more time researching her family tree.'

'Of course.'

'A misunderstanding,' he repeated.

'Nothing to be concerned about,' someone else murmured.

The housekeeper turned to Libby, as though searching for a different topic. 'Now, the other matter is your missing dog. We've all heard about him, and we'd like to help. Is there anything we can do, my dear?' The relief in the room at the change of subject was almost tangible. Full of enthusiasm, they debated the best way to find Bear, the suggestions ranging from advertisements in the local paper to the offer of a huge reward.

'If you could all check your sheds and outhouses, that would help, although we're almost sure he's been stolen.' Libby's voice wavered on the last words. She tried not to worry about Bear, but to concentrate on the group members. She'd detected undercurrents in the room she didn't quite understand.

She made a show of looking at her watch, promising to let them know as soon as there was progress in the search for Bear, and left, saying she needed to visit a few other people who may have seen him recently.

As they waved her away, she sensed a lightening of tension, as though at least one person in the room was glad to see her leave. She had the strangest feeling something important had happened, but no matter how many times she ran the conversation through her head, she couldn't think what she'd missed.

14

A BOX OF CHOCOLATES

Mandy's car in the drive was a welcome sight, when Libby returned to the cottage. The car belonged, officially, to the business, but it was Mandy's pride and joy. 'Mrs F, your fiancé said you'd be coming here.'

'My fian—? Oh, you mean Max.' Mandy always managed to make Libby laugh. This evening, there was something odd about her. It took Libby a moment or two to work out what was missing. 'Your hair!'

Mandy ignored the comment. 'I've got instructions to cheer you up. He's going to be away overnight. Apparently, he's chasing some leads to do with the stolen dogs and he doesn't want you feeling sad. He has Shipley with him, so you don't need to go over to the big house, and I'm here as his – what's the word? – his proxy, bearing gifts.' She led Libby into the kitchen, where a bottle of Libby's favourite red wine was prominently displayed next to a giant vase of flowers and a box of chocolates. 'Those are another company's chocolates. It didn't seem right to bring you a box of your own.' Mandy giggled.

She insisted Libby sit down. 'The dinner's in the oven. Have a glass of this and spill all the beans.'

'You know I can't...'

'Mrs F. This is me. How many mysteries have we worked on together? You know I won't blab.'

'Well, apart from Max, you're the only one I tell real secrets to. I know you won't let me down. But first, why the change of style? No black lipstick? No white face powder? Ponytail hair? What's going on?'

'Well spotted. I've had a makeover. Not sure I care for it, really.' Mandy tugged at her demure shift dress. 'I've been to Steve's end-of-year concert in London. Only just got back. Thought I wouldn't embarrass him in front of his posh musician friends.' She let out a peal of laughter. 'Needn't have bothered. They're a right scruffy bunch up at the College of Music.'

'Mad musicians, you mean?'

'You have no idea. Tomorrow, I'm getting back to normal. Steve said he hardly recognised me without my – er – my stuff.' Mandy and Steve had been together, barring quarrels, since Steve finished his studies at Wells Cathedral School. Things were clearly getting serious. 'He said he likes me grungy.' She settled in an armchair. 'Now, fill me in and I'll lend you the benefit of my medium-sized brain.'

Libby frowned. 'What did you mean, Max is chasing leads? What's he up to? Why didn't he ring?'

'You know what he's like. He was in a rush when I bumped into him. Said he'd ring you later, and not to worry.'

Max was notoriously bad at keeping Libby informed. He hated broadcasting his whereabouts, even to her. Still, maybe he was on to something. Perhaps he'd be back soon, bringing Bear.

'I hope he's taking care.'

'Course he is.'

A familiar knot of worry tied itself in Libby's stomach, but there was nothing she could do, except relate the events of the last couple of days to Mandy and wait to hear from Max. She took a swig of wine and dropped two comforting chocolates in her mouth at once.

* * *

Max did not telephone that evening. Libby waited until midnight, persuading a reluctant Fuzzy to join her on the sofa by hand-feeding cat treats. She did not want to be alone, tonight.

At last, knowing he was unlikely to call her so late, she sent a text:

Off to bed. Hope all's well. Shipley OK? Phone me tomorrow.

She steadfastly refused to use text speak.

She expected to toss and turn all night, worrying in turn about Bear and Max, but in fact, she slept soundly, and woke with a renewed determination to get to grips with her problems. There was no answering text from Max. Maybe his battery had run out? Unlikely. Max was an organised man. Meticulous, as he put it. She grinned at the memory. If only he'd told her where he was going.

She scrambled out of bed, showered and dressed, and ate a lonely breakfast. Not long to go until the wedding, she remembered. Her heart sank. Without Bear? Come on, Max. Tell me what's happening.

The phone rang. Startled, she fumbled it from her pocket and dropped it on the floor.

It was Joe. 'Sorry, did I wake you?' he asked.

She forced a smile into her voice. 'No. I thought – oh, nothing.' No need to worry Joe.

'Well, I've been looking into these stolen dog gangs.'

'Really? Isn't it a bit low-level for you, now you're a grand detective inspector?'

'Very funny. I just had a quick look at the files. I found another missing Carpathian Shepherd dog report.'

'You're kidding.' Libby's thoughts whirled. 'You mean, someone's deliberately targeting the breed?'

'Looks like it. They're rare in the UK, so it would be stretching coincidence a bit far if another was stolen randomly.'

'Is it local?'

'Sadly not. Hereford.'

'Isn't that in your new area?' Libby had a thought. 'Did you tell Max? He's gone off to talk to other owners, but he didn't tell me where he went.'

Joe tutted. 'Typical Dad. Bet you'll have a few choice words in his ear when he gets back. And yes, Hereford is in West Mercia. I'll be there shortly, and if I can help, I will. Unfortunately, it's highly unlikely we'll be able to offer any resources – but since when did you and Max need help?'

Libby thought aloud. 'He might have found out about it online. He's been googling dog theft. Do you have an address?'

'I do, but don't tell them I sent you.'

'Wouldn't dream of it.'

By the time the call ended, a smile had spread over Libby's face. No need to panic. If only Max were better at telling her what he was up to. She blamed his time on government work. Even though his skills were financial, she knew he'd sometimes put himself in harm's way. 'Need to know,' he called it. Libby would work on that habit when he returned.

Finishing her coffee, she spooned cat food into Fuzzy's bowl and thought about her business. She hadn't given Angela's news about Terence Marchant much thought. If he was back in town, and planning the opening of a rival establishment, she should act. She couldn't afford to lose business. Cakes and chocolates were her main source of income, and Mandy's apprenticeship depended on the business continuing. And what about Frank? He'd poured his life into the bakery.

Libby had met Marchant on several occasions and disliked him more every time. He was rich, had no taste, and always looked Libby up and down as though imagining her with no clothes on. She shivered at the thought.

Should she visit him and appeal to his better nature? She dismissed that idea. He'd use the 'this is business, not personal' defence. No, she must fight fire with fire. Frank's bakery was hugely popular in Exham, and people loved Libby's chocolates. Satisfied customers would be the best weapons to fight a threat to the business.

She rang Angela. 'We're going to have a party. A huge affair. We'll get the press involved, with giveaways and raffles, and cake decorating competitions. It'll be the biggest event Exham's ever seen, promoting all our wares. We'll scare Terence Marchant off, before he's even begun.'

'Then, we need to hurry. His place is opening in two weeks.'

It took Angela no time at all to start planning the party. Libby arrived at the house to find her friend, fingers poised over a laptop, with a pile of printouts of various lists. 'I knew you'd be the right person to organise things,' Libby admitted. 'I'm having trouble with my own wedding.'

'Not having second thoughts again, are you?' Angela glared over half-moon specs.

Libby held up a hand. 'Definitely not. We were going for a day in a couple of weeks time, but I don't see how we can have a wonderful day without Bear. Maybe we should wait a while longer. There's no hurry. I'll see what Max thinks.'

'Why don't you concentrate on getting Bear back? I'll rope Mandy in to help with the party. I thought a wine and chocolate theme would go down well. In fact, I've got an idea that might work...'

Libby laughed. 'I knew I could trust you. I'll leave it in your hands.'

'Just set the budget and I'll do the rest. And, tell Max you want to postpone the wedding for a while. He'll understand. He waited long enough for you decide you wanted to marry him.'

A weight lifted from Libby's shoulders. 'You're right. He already said there's no hurry. Why am I getting so wound up? I'll talk to him next time. Oh—' She remembered he'd disappeared. 'I think I need to track him down.'

Angela pointed to the door. 'Go.'

15

TEA

Margery Halfstead's head ached and her chest hurt. The doctors told her she was lucky, the knife hadn't hit any important organs, but had slid off her ribcage. She'd endured seven stitches to the wound and an overnight stay in hospital. 'I want to see my husband,' she told the nurse, as she was woken at some ridiculously early hour to have her blood pressure taken.

'I'm sure you can, a little later, if the doctor's happy with your vital signs.'

'Vital signs, my eye.' Margery swung her legs out of bed. 'The doctor said it was just a scratch. I'm getting up.'

'Now, wait until you've had breakfast, why don't you?'

'Nonsense.'

Margery pulled back a curtain to find an elderly lady lying in the next bed, mouth hanging open, barely conscious. Margery replaced the curtain. The nurse raised her eyebrows, shrugged and left her alone, while Margery searched the tiny wardrobe at her bedside, looking for clothes. The dress she'd been wearing was missing. She clicked her tongue. The police had taken it for evidence. She contorted her body, stretching her arms back the short distance she could reach, given the pain of stitches in her side. She winced, struggling to untie the knotted string at the back of her flimsy NHS-issue nightgown, admitted defeat, and shuffled across the ward.

A sign in the corridor pointed the way to two other wards, but the names meant nothing to Margery. She took a chance and pushed open the nearest door. A nurse looked up. 'I'm sorry, you're in the wrong ward. The women's beds are next door.'

'I want to see my husband.'

'I'm sorry?'

'My husband. He's in here, I think.' She looked along the row of beds. 'Mr Halfstead.'

The nurse's expression changed. 'Oh, William's your husband? He's over there, by the window. Such a lovely gentleman.'

Margery frowned. She hated this modern habit young people had, of calling everyone by their first name. 'I'll see Mr Halfstead now, thank you.'

'Well, it's not visiting time, but I suppose, if you're here too.' She looked more closely at Margery's face. 'Are you feeling faint?'

'Most certainly not. I just wish to see my husband.' She was not sure where this determination had come from. All she knew was she had to make things right with William.

She stalked down the ward. William lay asleep. He looked old and tired. His face was grey. Margery, a rush of affection bringing a tear to her eyes, kissed his cheek. 'I'm so sorry,' she whispered.

His eyes flickered. He opened his mouth and said something his wife couldn't catch. She leaned closer. 'I'm here, William. It's me.'

A smile flitted over his face. 'Milly,' he croaked.

The words might as well have been a punch in the stomach. Margery staggered back. 'Milly? Who's Milly?'

William's eyes had closed once more. Margery clapped her hands over her mouth, afraid she might be sick. Mouth trembling, she turned away from the bed and shuffled back across the ward. She could hardly see the nurse for the tears filling her eyes. She'd been right. William had other women. Not just Annabel. Someone called Milly, as well.

Out in the corridor, she leaned against the wall, struggling to catch her breath. She must get home. She couldn't spend another minute in this hateful place. She longed to be in her own cosy home, surrounded by her precious possessions, while she thought this through.

She shook her head, struggling to clear it. Who could she call, to get some clothes sent in? The intruder, stabbing her at her own front door, seemed like no more than a bad dream, except for the pain of those stitches. No matter what became of her, she wanted to be in her own home. She hurried back to her bedside, grabbed the phone and business card from her bag, and punched in the number. Libby Forest would help.

* * *

Despite her determination, it wasn't easy for Margery to convince the staff she was ready to leave hospital. As the nurse explained, with forced cheerfulness, a doctor would be in to see her, but he was very busy this morning.

'I can discharge myself, can't I?'

The nurse squirmed. 'You can, but you'll have to sign a disclaimer.'

Margery fixed the nurse with a steely gaze. 'Then bring me whatever I should sign, as soon as possible.'

She waited, sitting by her bed, staring into space. Her world had crashed around her ears and she wanted to go home. How long would she be imprisoned in this place? It seemed the nursing staff were in no hurry to let her go, and she was losing the energy to fight. Just as she was about to roll back into bed and cry her eyes out, the nurse returned, with Libby in tow.

The nurse pointed to Margery. 'Please take her,' she muttered. 'You've saved my sanity.'

Even so, it was an hour before Margery was finally allowed to leave, clutching a paper bag containing painkillers and wearing a skirt and jumper she would never have chosen for herself. Libby confessed they were the first clothes she'd laid her hands on. At least she'd had no trouble finding the key under a loose paving stone, just as Margery had directed.

Margery sat in silence on the way home, relieved to find her companion did not insist on talking. No doubt she mistook Margery's mood of seething fury for a reaction to the trauma. Margery had met the first tentative enquiries about William with a short, 'He's on the mend,' in the tone of voice that forbids further enquiry.

Libby helped her through the front door, although she felt perfectly capable of walking alone, and made a cup of tea, asking questions as they drank. Margery tried to remember what had happened. 'I wanted to talk to you, that day, before – before I answered the door – because I needed to clear my head. I was starting to think all kinds of stupid things.'

'Tell me what happened. Who was at the door?'

Margery screwed her face up with effort. 'I've been trying to remember. You see, I only got a quick glimpse and she was wearing a big coat and a headscarf —'

'She?' Libby interrupted. 'You mean, it was a woman?'

'Why, yes. But she was big. Not tall, exactly, but well built. Strong.'

'How old was she?'

'Hard to tell. She was wearing big glasses and a headscarf, with just a little dark hair poking out round the sides. That's how I could tell it was a woman.'

Margery's lip trembled and Libby poured more tea. 'You don't need to talk about it any more , just yet.'

'I've been thinking, and I'm sure she didn't really want to kill me, you know. It was just the one blow, and it wasn't aimed at my heart. She could have stabbed me again. I think she was expecting to see William, and I took her by surprise.' Margery's determined smile wavered. 'I think I'm going to have a little sleep soon, if you don't mind. Thank you for bringing me home, but I'd like to be alone.'

'Of course, if that's what you'd prefer. I'll let myself out and come back later, to see how you're getting on.'

Margery finished the tea, feeling a little better. Maybe Libby Forest wasn't such a fool, but Margery had wanted to get rid of her. She didn't want to think about the woman who'd stabbed her. It was only a scratch, after all. No real damage done. She cared more about William's behaviour. If he was having an affair, she had to know.

She climbed the stairs, slowly, feeling the stitches in her side pulling painfully on the bruised skin. William's clothes hung neatly in his wardrobe, or were folded in drawers. Margery insisted on a tidy home.

A twinge of guilt prompted a moment's hesitation as she felt in his pockets, but she hardened her heart. William deserved it. Besides, she had to know the truth, no matter how much it hurt.

There was nothing out of the ordinary in any of the pockets; just the odd bus ticket and imperial mint. William wouldn't be so foolish as to keep evidence of his treachery where Margery would be likely to look.

She sat on the bed, and thought. Where did he go, that she did not follow? Where might he hide things?

A slow smile spread over Margery's face. Of course. The shed, that was it. William insisted every man had to own a shed. His wife was not allowed to clean – or even tidy – the small wooden building in the garden. The shed was William's den.

'Right,' Margery said aloud. 'That's where it will be.' She had no idea what she expected to find, but the urge to know the truth kept her going.

She searched through pots of nails sorted by size, and cans of half-finished paint. They yielded nothing out of the ordinary. Margery pushed them aside, and pulled out the glass jars arranged behind them in a row on a metal shelf. Odds and ends, that's all she found. Coins, buttons, a broken ruler, and several pencil stubs. Until, almost ready to give up the hunt, she picked up the last jar. It seemed to be full of cotton wool.

Margery frowned. What in the world would William be doing with cotton wool?

She tipped the jar's contents onto the only table in the shed, her fingers scrabbling. In the middle of the bundle, a key gleamed.

Her fingers trembled as she picked it up and looked around for something to unlock.

Next to the table, she saw a tarpaulin covered chest, placed instead of a chair. Margery pulled aside the cover. The box was ornate – a perfect match for the key. It was elaborately carved from some foreign wood – sandalwood, Margery guessed, sniffing the faint, pleasant wood fragrance.

She slipped the key in the lock. It turned smoothly. She took a deep breath and opened the lid.

* * *

When Libby returned, tired and dispirited after two hours distributing lost-dog posters in a nearby town, she found Margery on the sofa, gripping a small wooden box, sobbing as though her heart would break.

'What is it? Are you in pain? Shall I call the doctor?'

Margery shook her head. She held out the box. Libby took it, hesitant, expecting Margery to snap out one of her sharp comments. Instead, Margery covered her face with her hands.

Libby lowered herself to sit at Margery's side and opened the box. Inside were a tiny pair of bootees, a baby's white nightgown, and a folded muslin square. 'For the baby,' Margery whispered.

'Baby?' Libby touched the bootees, delicately. 'Whose baby?'

Margery cleared her throat. 'Ours. We were going to have a baby, but something went wrong. I never knew William had bought these things. He didn't tell me. He must have hidden them, all those years ago.' Her voice quavered. 'He hid them so as not to upset me.'

One by one, she lifted the clothes and handed them to Libby. 'Look.' She showed Libby a small, much folded piece of paper. 'He wanted a little girl. I wanted a boy. I had a list of boys' names, but this is his.' There were just two names on the paper: Margery and Milly. 'Milly was the name he wanted for our baby.'

Libby supplied copious amounts of tea and sympathy. Margery blew her nose, folded the baby clothes neatly in their tissue paper and began to talk, relief clearly making her garrulous. 'I've been so silly. How could I have mistrusted him?' She gave a watery smile. 'I always thought William was too good for me, that's the truth. He's such an attractive man. I've never quite believed my luck that he wanted to marry me. When I get him home, I'm going to spoil him rotten. I'll even let him go fishing again.'

She locked the box, smoothing the surface with gentle hands.

'He stopped fishing after that last competition. He was sure he'd won. He caught an enormous rainbow trout, over six pounds, he reckoned, but the scales let him down. He said they were weighted. I told him not to bother with a club where there were cheats.'

The colour had returned to her cheeks. 'I know he misses his mornings by the water. I'll buy him some more fishing kit, that's what I'll do. He'll like that.'

Libby slipped away, leaving Margery searching out old fishing leaflets from a magazine rack.

16

CHERRY BAKEWELLS

Libby had never understood Margery's conviction that Annabel and William were having an affair. Annabel was so much younger than him, and had showed no signs of pining for him. Libby wasn't at all surprised to discover it was all in Margery's imagination.

However, his uncharacteristic disappearance, when he was supposedly in charge of the schoolboys, remained unsolved. Where had he gone? Could he have been with Beryl? Nicotine, Libby had read, can act fast. It was perfectly possible to imagine William offering Beryl a drink of whisky containing enough poison to kill her within minutes.

Was William really the killer? He'd had the opportunity, but what was his motive? Libby hadn't yet tried to uncover whether he had the knowledge to distil nicotine, but he had worked all his life in teaching. He was nobody's fool.

The only fact that pointed suspicion firmly away from him was the attack on his wife. No one could dispute his alibi, as he was in hospital, but Libby's fertile brain conjured up various ways he could still be responsible. An accomplice, perhaps? Someone working with William for some unknown purpose? Or perhaps, even if the older man had no interest in Annabel, he could be having an affair with someone else. What about the mysterious volunteer Margery saw? Had the police tracked her down?

Libby longed to talk it over with Max. If only he'd get in touch. She hesitated, tempted to find out where he'd gone and follow him.

As she hesitated, her phone pinged.

Max. It was almost as though he'd heard her thoughts. The text was brief, but at least he was in contact:

On the trail. Terrible reception here. Will contact if any news. Shipley helping.

Libby almost cried with relief. Max was fine, just busy and out of range. She hadn't thought of that. A niggling voice whispered that he couldn't have been out of range all the time, and she'd have something to say about his silence when he came home. Still, if only he could find Bear, things would be perfect. She grinned, anticipating a short argument, followed by an enjoyable reconciliation.

Suddenly full of hope, her spirits leapt. She would concentrate on enquiries into Beryl's murder and the attack on Margery. She wanted to prove William innocent, for Margery's sake, but she reminded herself of Joe's advice to follow the evidence, even if it led in a direction she disliked.

She planned to follow up the reason for the school party's presence in the castle on the morning of Beryl's murder. Was it a coincidence? William had been responsible for arranging the visit.

She telephoned Jason Franklin's school. The receptionist was reluctant to make an immediate appointment, but Libby was ready with hints at possible consequences for the school if the students' supervision at the castle had been inadequate. The receptionist suddenly found a window in the headteacher's diary. She could see Libby straight away.

Libby ended the call and set off for the school. Max would be proud of her assertiveness.

The school was a comprehensive of over a thousand students, spread over a large campus backing onto open fields. It seemed a pleasant place to go to school, although Libby's quick googling of its most recent Ofsted report showed it 'required improvement' in several areas. The sixth form, apparently, needed more 'stretching'.

Libby left her car in the staff car park, pressed a buzzer, and asked to be admitted. She got a kick out of showing her police credentials to the receptionist, who reluctantly disappeared to check whether the head teacher was available.

Mrs Bass, the head teacher, arrived without unnecessary delay. She was an upright, smart looking lady, probably within a year or two of retirement age. 'How can I help?' she asked, her manner business-like rather than warm, as she ushered Libby into her office. 'Is this to do with that unfortunate death at the castle? My boys were very shocked, as you can imagine. I've organised counselling, should any of them require it, but so far, they seem to be coping remarkably well. We have a strong and supportive environment in this school.'

'I'm sure that will have helped,' Libby said, aiming for diplomacy. She was disconcerted by memories of her own headmistress's study. How did people manage to build such a forbidding aura, even in rooms barely different from a doctor's surgery or solicitor's office?

She coughed and concentrated on the business at hand. 'I work with the police as a civilian officer,' she explained, 'and I'm gathering background information about the day of the castle visit. The boys who were present have given statements, and I was there when Jason Franklin was interviewed. Today, I'm just trying to understand how they came to be in the castle that day. It was a little unusual, because the castle was officially closed.'

The head teacher nodded. 'It was a special occasion. As you will know, Jason's father is our local MP. He gives an extraordinary degree of support to the school.' I bet he does, Libby thought. Best way to make sure his son gets preferential treatment.

As though reading her mind, the head teacher continued. 'That does not mean Jason gains any kind of advantage over the other students.' Mrs Bass shot a look at Libby that defied her to argue. 'Thomas – Mr Franklin – also supports the Trust that manages the castle. They were willing to allow an exceptional visit, on this one occasion.'

'Of course.' Libby let it go for now. Mrs Bass's coolness made it clear she was not interested in sharing gossip, but a spot of colour in her cheeks alerted Libby's instincts. How well did the head-teacher know the MP? She chose her words with care. 'Apparently, Jason was chosen to take part in the short drama. You know, writing a script and speaking to Miss Nightingale to discuss the fictional menu.'

'That was down to Mr Halfstead. He organised a short essay competition among the boys – something about the plight of domestic servants in Victorian times, I believe – and Jason produced the best entry. The visit had been planned for a different day, but when Jason discovered he would be absent that day, his father requested a special outing. Jason was due to visit Oxford University. Several of our students apply each year to the pinnacles of academia, and I'm rather proud to say that two boys were successful last year – one to read physics at Cambridge, the other, classics at Oxford. Jason is hoping to take a history degree.'

Mrs Bass sounded so pleased with herself that Libby could not resist asking, 'The school's improved since the most recent Ofsted report, then?'

The head teacher's manner cooled. 'I was not in charge when that inspection took place. I was employed subsequently, and my remit has been to improve the weaker areas of the school. I'm pleased to say that yes, the school has indeed improved. We expect Jason and one or two others of our current sixth form to make us even more proud, this year.'

'So, Jason is a star pupil?'

'One of them.'

The receptionist entered, bearing refreshments on a tray. Two cherry Bakewell tarts looked suspiciously like Libby's own work.

The head teacher, perhaps noticing Libby's smile, allowed her manner to soften a little. 'Your fame as a cook has travelled before you, Mrs Forest. Perhaps we will be able to persuade you to give a talk to some of our students, one day.'

Clever woman. How could Libby possibly refuse such a request, if she wanted more co-operation within the school? No wonder Mrs Bass had improved the school's performance. She was someone to reckon with. 'I'll look at my diary,' Libby promised. "I'm sure I can help.'

The head teacher, with an air of satisfaction, stirred her tea and took a neat bite from a cake. Libby seized the moment of rapport to find out more about Thomas Franklin. 'I expect it's useful to have the MP's son doing so well in your school...'

'He's certainly a credit to his father.' She positively beamed. 'Thomas Franklin really is a most interesting man. He's only been the local MP for two years, but he's lived in the area much longer. He's a most amusing speaker. He drew quite a crowd when he opened our annual fête.' Libby had seen the man on television talk shows, where he certainly knew how to charm the audience. Judging by the headteacher's increased animation, Libby suspected Mrs Bass's interest went beyond the professional.

That, however, did not imply anything suspicious about the man's request for a change of date for the castle visit. That seemed to have nothing to do with the headteacher. Once again, the key seemed to be William Halfstead. Libby turned the conversation back in that direction. 'Mr Halfstead used to teach here, I believe.'

'Before my time, but yes. He retired shortly after I was appointed.'

'Was that early retirement?'

Mrs Bass let her gaze slide sideways. 'A year or so, I believe.'

Libby silently noted the head teacher's discomfort. 'Forgive me for asking, but was there any particular reason why he was encouraged to retire?'

'No scandal, if that's what you're suggesting. If there had been, Mr Halfstead would most certainly not be allowed to guide our students around the castle. No, it was simply a change in ethos and methods. I had to bring the school up to date, in some ways. For example, more account taken of studying contemporary texts in history lessons, and rather less in the way of dressing up.' The head teacher stopped talking, a little abruptly. Libby had the impression she'd been franker than she intended.

Libby's brain buzzed as she left. The head teacher's careful words had not quite concealed her disapproval of William Halfstead. Did that make him a more likely suspect, or was it simply a difference of opinion about teaching methods? Then, there was the MP, charming the headteacher and willing to use his position on behalf of his son. Had he any sort of hold over Mr Halfstead? And if so, what relevance would that have to Beryl Nightingale's death?

* * *

During Libby's interview with the head teacher, DCI Morrison had sent a text inviting Libby to a case conference to consider progress in Beryl Nightingale's murder enquiry. She arrived, breathless, in time to catch a full toxicology report that finally, and definitively, confirmed the cause of Beryl's death as nicotine poisoning.

DC Gemma Humberstone's glance at Libby was brief and unfriendly, and when Libby was asked to update the room on any information she'd gleaned in the past couple of days, the young officer's expression took on a hard edge. 'I'm aware that I need to be sensitive about any investigation into an MP,' Libby ended her report, and peeked at her watch. She'd arranged to spend the evening at a concert in Wells, where the performers included Mandy's boyfriend, Steve, an old pupil at the cathedral school.

DCI Morrison stepped in. 'A good point. Gemma, perhaps you could follow up Mrs Forest's excellent work.' The look Gemma shot in Libby's direction was pure fury.

Ian Smith looked from one to the other, a satisfied smile playing on his lips. At first Libby was puzzled, then a thought struck her. He really doesn't like women. He wants both Gemma and me to fall on our faces. If only Gemma didn't resent my involvement so much, I might be able to help her. I've come across many Ian Smiths before. Notably in the shape of her own husband, now deceased.

The DCI was still talking. 'We need to review our hypotheses at this point. We know Miss Nightingale was murdered, via something she ate or drank. She would not have been able to smoke sufficient cigarettes, or chew sufficient tobacco, to cause death. We need to consider whether there is the possibility of a self-inflicted poisoning, however unlikely a method this would appear to be. Mrs Forest, you knew the victim better than any of us. Would you believe her capable of suicide?'

Libby considered. 'She was a rather sad person, with a hidden drink problem. When I say hidden, I mean no one talked about it. However, residents all seem to be aware she drank. If she killed herself, I would ask, why now? The drink problem is long standing.'

Several nods in the room supported Libby's conclusion. Emboldened, she continued. 'A possible explanation may be the way she left her job. I've heard conflicting reports. Some say she retired – she was well over retirement age – while others hint at a query over accounting issues.'

Morrison nodded. 'Gemma, that's another one for you to follow up with the racing stables – the accounts belonged to them. Any other theories at this stage, anyone?'

Gemma Humberstone jotted something in her notebook, saying, 'I'd like to know more about William Halfstead. We shouldn't write him off as a suspect, simply because he's since had a heart attack. He was at the castle, and responsible for the presence of the schoolchildren.'

Libby raised a hand, then lowered it, blushing like a child. 'His wife mentioned he was out of sight around the time of Beryl's death. She suggested he might have been pursuing one of the other volunteers at the time.'

Ian Smith spluttered coffee on the floor. 'At his age? Chance would be a fine thing.'

Morrison bestowed a cold stare on his subordinate, and Libby caught a glimpse of the steel beneath the senior officer's gentle exterior. 'Because you're such a catch, Ian?'

'Come on, sir. The man must be seventy. Who was he after? Another geriatric?' A couple of young male officers tittered, but DCI Morrison's eyes narrowed.

Ian Smith's heading for trouble.

Gemma glanced at Libby and raised her eyebrow the tiniest fraction. Warmed by this show of feminine solidarity, however mild, Libby explained Margery's theory that her husband might be having an affair with Annabel.

DCI Morrison nodded. 'He's still at the top of our list, then. We'll need a proper statement from his wife. I suppose she's in the clear?'

'Judging by the amount of nicotine in the victim's tissues,' Gemma was glancing through the pathologist's report, 'it's likely the poison was administered less than an hour before death. There was enough of it in her body to kill a horse. So, Margery Halfstead would have been able to administer it, as would anyone who knew the victim. If she hadn't been attacked, I'd want to keep her on the list. Could the stabbing have been a pretence?' She looked at Libby, eyebrows raised.

Libby doubted Margery's ability to plan and carry out such a deception. 'I heard the attack and it sounded genuine enough. But, it's possible.'

'We'll keep her in mind,' DCI Morrison confirmed, 'just in case.'

PC Smith had been nodding while Gemma spoke, as though he'd attained some insight. He sounded triumphant. 'The killer must have been in the castle.'

Morrison raised a weary eyebrow. 'No,' he said, with a show of patience. 'The poison could have been introduced into the victim's alcohol at any time.'

Even Ian Smith recognised the disdain in his boss's voice, and slouched down in a chair.

'By the way, sir,' Gemma was frowning. 'We haven't managed to trace a woman seen at the castle. Mrs Halfstead mentioned seeing her upstairs. On a normal day, it would be impossible to track her down, but as the castle was closed except for the students, she was either there officially, helping with the cleaning, or she sneaked in. So far, no one seems to know who she is. It may not be important, and she was upstairs when the victim died, but...'

Several heads had jerked up. A rare smile brightened DCI Morrison's face. 'Well done, Gemma. Quite right. She need have nothing to do with the murder, but I don't like loose ends. Chase that up, will you? Find out who else saw our mystery woman, and get me a name.'

DCI Morrison tapped papers on the table, indicating the conference was drawing to a close. 'No one's ruled out, yet. Anyone in the castle that morning could have done the deed. A friend or neighbour who had access to Miss Nightingale's house – they could have dropped the poison in a bottle of her favourite tipple at any time. What was her favourite, by the way?'

'Whisky.' Libby's response caused a general groan.

'Could have been there for years, then.' The muscles of Morrison's habitually glum face drooped even further. 'Still, we'll bear it in mind. Ian, start talking to the neighbours. Gemma, speak to the housekeeper at the castle. Don't forget to liaise, you two, as some neighbours may also be volunteers.' Gemma's grim expression betrayed her lack of enthusiasm for working with Ian Smith, but the boss made no comment. 'Mrs Forest, thank you for your help so far. Any more ideas are very welcome.'

Libby turned to leave, just as Ian Smith leered at Gemma. 'Come on then, babe. Let's liaise.'

No wonder Gemma Humberstone had a defensive attitude. If Smith wasn't careful, he'd get himself in trouble for comments like that.

17

ORANGE JUICE

Libby was glad to fill the evening with a concert and avoid the long lonely hours of darkness while Max was away. She slid into a wooden pew in Wells Cathedral, next to Mandy. Angela, Steve's aunt, sat on Libby's left side. Mandy's Goth makeup had reappeared, and she'd topped the look with a black velvet hat that Libby secretly coveted.

Awed by the splendour of the cathedral's arches and the expectant hush from the audience, Libby waited until the orchestra began tuning their instruments before whispering, under the cover of the noise, 'I've heard from Max. He's fine, so I'll leave him alone to get on with his enquiries. He managed perfectly well before he knew me. I don't know why I was so anxious.'

'Wedding nerves?'

'Maybe. No news of Bear, I'm afraid.'

'Look on the bright side,' Mandy urged. 'The gang aren't killing dogs, they're stealing valuable animals. Max is on the case. He'll find him.'

'Hope you're right.' Libby wriggled. 'Anyway, I'm determined not to worry about Bear, or anything else, this evening. I'm going to enjoy the music.'

Mandy giggled. 'I won't tell you what I heard on the grapevine, then.'

The conductor tapped his baton and the orchestra began to play.

'What did you hear?'

A woman in the row behind shushed her. Mandy shrugged. 'Sorry, tell you at the interval.'

Libby's brain raced and she listened with only half an ear to the music. What could Mandy know? Was it about Bear? She discarded that idea. If Mandy had known something, she would have been bursting to tell. Perhaps she'd heard more gossip about Beryl or the Halfsteads.

At last, the final notes wafted to the ceiling. Libby grabbed Mandy's arm. 'You wretch, I've been on tenterhooks. What do you know?'

Mandy wrinkled her nose. 'Sorry, that was bad timing. When I was in the bakery, we had a visit from the man who's just moved into that big house that's been empty for months. You know, up in Millionaire's Rise?' Libby nodded. Everyone knew that street in Exham. Every house in it was way above the average resident's budget.

'He stayed in the shop for ages. Seems like he wants to get to know people. A bit smarmy, if you know what I mean, but Gladys from the flower shop seemed to like him.'

'She likes all men.'

'Whatever.' Libby winced at the expression as Mandy continued. 'Anyway, this isn't just gossip about her. The man – called himself Henderson, I think. That's right, Patrick Henderson.'

Libby wanted to scream. Would Mandy never get to the point? She bit her lip and waited.

'He said he'd come to see Beryl, because she used to work in his racing stables, but there was no reply at her house. Well, you can imagine. Gladys got all excited, telling him about Beryl dying at the castle, and how there was a rumour she'd left her job under a cloud, and did the man know anything about it?' She paused for breath.

'Go on,' Angela urged, as gripped as Libby, 'before they come back for the second half.'

'In a nutshell, this man said he supposed he could tell her because, he said "Beryl's dead and you can't slander the dead, can you, ha ha"' Mandy wrinkled her nose in disgust. 'Anyway, that rumour was true. Beryl used money from the business to make investments, but they'd all gone wrong before she could replace the cash, and the end of year audit uncovered the discrepancies.'

Angela drew in a long breath. 'So, she was stealing from the firm. Who would ever have believed it of Beryl?'

'What's more,' Mandy finished in a rush, 'because she lost the money she was dismissed and she was stony broke apart from the few bob from the state pension.'

It was time for the second part of the concert, and Steve stepped forward with two colleagues to play a saxophone trio; a setting of Alexander's Ragtime Band that soon had the audience tapping their feet. Mandy switched her attention to her boyfriend, her mouth slightly ajar, cheeks pink with excitement. Libby glanced to her other side, where Angela's rapt expression mimicked Mandy's, and grinned. For the moment, both her companions had forgotten the murder victim and the missing dog.

At the end of the evening, Libby turned down Angela's invitation to celebrate at her house. 'I'd love to, but I need to think about Mandy's information. If Beryl was broke and worried, that might mean she was drinking more.'

'Drowning her sorrows,' Mandy murmured, most of her attention still on Steve. Libby grinned. An idea was forming at the back of her mind.

* * *

Next morning, Libby was alone as Mandy had stayed with her aunt. Her lonely breakfast of orange juice and toast was interrupted by a ring at the doorbell. Libby leapt to open the door, excited, expecting to see Max, with Bear in tow alongside Shipley.

She flung open the door and smothered a groan. Gemma Humberstone was the last person she wanted to see.

The detective constable opened her mouth, but closed it again. Libby knew her face was a wreck. She hadn't even showered or combed her hair. Trying to appear calm, she took a deep breath and fixed a welcoming smile to her face. 'You'd better come in.'

She led DC Humberstone through to the kitchen, but the young woman refused an offer of tea. She looked uncomfortable, fidgeting and biting her lip. 'I wanted to make a suggestion, Mrs Forest, but I don't want to intrude.'

'I could do with some good news, to be honest.'

'Well, I have an appointment with Jason Franklin's father. He's requested – well insisted on – a meeting. He's not happy. I thought you might like to come along.'

'I certainly would.' An interview with the MP was just the tonic she needed, whatever the excuse, and the DCs offer felt like a small olive branch. 'Give me just a minute.'

Escaping, Libby threw water on her face, whizzed a brush

over her teeth and dragged on trousers and a jumper. Feeling slightly more human, she returned to the kitchen. 'I'm sorry to make you wait. I overslept.' She bit her tongue, annoyed that she sounded defensive.

As she pulled on a coat, her phone pinged with another text from Max:

In Hereford. Hopeful. Talk soon xx

Thomas Franklin was in his constituency surgery, close to the castle. Of average height, he carried himself with the assurance of a man who'd studied at Eton or Harrow. His carefully maintained shock of thick hair, the colour a vivid chestnut, could not possibly be natural, and his skin was deeply tanned to a colour that, in this part of the world, must be due either to a succession of foreign holidays or chemical assistance.

He made a great show of checking his watch and threw a pointed glance at the small band of petitioners sitting, cramped, on crowded chairs round the edges of the room. 'Come into my office. I can only give you a few minutes.'

He settled himself into a leather office chair and waved his visitors to a pair of small, hard chairs. There was no offer of refreshment. 'I gather you wish to discuss this business at the castle. As you can imagine, I'm not at all happy about my son's involvement, and I've made my feelings clear to the headmistress. I expect schoolchildren to be kept safe, not exposed to upsetting matters. Where was the man in charge? He seems to have abandoned the party and left them with his totally unqualified wife. My son may well be traumatised.'

Gemma avoided Libby's eye. 'Be that as it may,' she said, 'my job is to find out what happened.'

'Jason told you. He was talking on that ridiculous speaker tube, when this woman died.' The man's voice rose. 'The poor lad was actually speaking to her.'

'Yes, he told me what happened when I spoke to him at the castle. Mrs Forest was also present. I would like to add that your son is not under any suspicion. The students are currently viewed as unfortunate bystanders.' Libby admired the police officer's diplomacy.

The MP's bluster faded a little. He leaned back in his chair, raised his eyes to the ceiling, and steepled short, stubby fingers together. 'I am keen this should all be cleared up as quickly as possible. I assume you have a suspect. I hear William Halfstead is under suspicion.'

Libby listened closely, her eyes on the floor.

'I'm so sorry, I'm afraid I can't share that information at this stage.' Gemma spoke formally.

The MP frowned, used to having his own way. 'I'd be grateful,' he went on, 'if you'd keep me abreast of your enquiries. On behalf of my constituents, you know.'

'I will make sure you're kept informed when appropriate, sir. May I say, we're most grateful for the interest you're taking in the matter. We want to clear it up as soon as possible.'

'Of course, of course.' He sounded tetchy. 'Who was this woman? Brenda, was it?'

'Beryl. Beryl Nightingale. A volunteer at the castle.'

'Well, I'm always pleased to hear of members of the public doing their bit for the community. She was a friend of Mr Halfstead's, I believe?'

Gemma said nothing. The MP looked at his watch again. 'Well, I must get on. Plenty of problems to solve in the constituency surgery today. Thank you for putting my mind at rest that you have matters in hand. Wouldn't like my son to be more nervous than he is already. He has important exams coming up.'

Libby and Gemma were waved out. As she left, Libby glanced back, to see the MP watching them intently. Libby replayed the conversation in her head. He seemed very interested in William Halfstead.

They climbed back into the police car. 'Well, what do you make of that?' Gemma asked.

'An over-protective father?' Libby suggested. 'And boiling for a fight with the police.'

Gemma nodded. 'Exactly.'

She twisted round, ready to reverse the car out of its space. 'Thank you for coming. I wanted to apologise.'

'Oh?' Libby stayed non-committal.

'Yes. Ian Smith told me you impeded his enquiries in the matter of the poisoned cyclists. It happened before I joined the local police service, so I didn't know the details. Yesterday, we had a little leaving do for DI Ramshore and he told me the true story.'

Libby took a deep breath, controlling a burst of anger. How dare Ian Smith tell lies about her? 'No problem. That man's a menace. I don't envy you, having to work with him. He's always been difficult, but he seems to be getting more misogynistic, recently.'

Gemma swung the car expertly round the narrow corners of the A39, clicking her tongue as she was forced to slow behind a tractor. 'His third wife left him in the summer. I think he has a problem with women. Anyway, I'd better get back. Thanks again.'

Libby's smile was grim. Ian Smith needed to be taught a lesson. She wasn't sure how to manage it, but one day...

Meanwhile, she had other plans. Tired of waiting to hear

from Max, she decided to follow Bear's trail herself. She wouldn't stay at home, doing nothing, any longer. As the tractor pulled over to let the line of traffic through, Libby made up her mind. She'd set off for Hereford as soon as she could.

18

SAUSAGE ROLLS

Libby followed a scenic route to Hereford that led beside the River Wye, picturesque woodland towering on either side, but she wasted no time admiring the view. Her thoughts were all of Bear.

A search of Facebook had uncovered posts from the missing dog's owner, with a picture of a dog who looked remarkably like Bear, playing with a small red-headed child outside a farmhouse. Libby, reaching the address Joe supplied, recognised the house. The farmyard was swept clean, and the barns and outhouses well cared for. A young woman opened the door, with not one but two red-haired children in tow. From their dungarees, identical in design, except that one was blue and the other green, Libby deduced they were boy twins. They looked about three years old.

'Mrs Brant?'

The woman nodded. 'Can I help?'

Libby read hope in the woman's eyes. 'I'm afraid I don't have any news of your dog.'

The spark died and Mrs Brant sighed. 'How do you know about him?'

'I've lost a similar animal.'

'Really? You'd better come in.' Libby followed as Mrs Brant shooed her two small boys into a cluttered room, the carpet spread with toys. She turned the sound on the television down to a murmur. 'Sorry. They love Peter Rabbit. It will keep them happy while we talk. Thank heaven for iPlayer.' She waved Libby to an ancient, squashy sofa. 'They're missing the dog terribly. Well, me and my husband, too, of course. Barry's away today, gone to buy a new ram.' She shot a quizzical glance at Libby. 'How did you know about us?'

Libby remembered she was here unofficially. 'Facebook. I wondered if you had any information?'

The woman moved over to a window that looked out towards the back of the house. 'Not really. Domino – that's the dog's name – was out in the garden one minute, and next time I looked, he was gone. We thought he'd just escaped, but we checked the fences, and there were no gaps. We hoped he'd show up in a day or two, but no one's seen him. We put his photo on Facebook, and everyone's sympathetic, but there's no information. We're starting to think he's gone for good.'

Libby told the young woman about Bear. 'It seems there's a market for Carpathians.'

'They're wonderful sheepdogs, but we keep Domino as a pet. He's so gentle with the boys. They crawl all over him, and pull his tail, and he never even growls.'

* * *

The farm visit hadn't taken Libby any further forward. She left Mrs Brant and her two boys, promising to keep in touch, and drove the few miles into the city. She'd refused coffee at the farm, guessing the busy mother had plenty to do, but she was gasping for coffee. It wouldn't do any harm to ask a few questions of local people.

Parking in the city turned out to be easier than she'd expected, and she was soon trekking from one shop to another, showing posters of Bear and asking everyone who'd listen if they'd heard about any missing dogs.

She drew a blank in her first target, a pharmacy, and had little better luck in the estate agency next door. 'I don't know about missing dogs, but I can show you the most likely area to keep one, if you're interested in moving?'

Libby gave the young man full marks for salesmanship, but had no time to waste. There was a small café nearby, so she elbowed the door open. It was deserted, apart from a blonde waitress who flicked crumbs from tables, from time to time admiring herself in the mirror at the back of the shop.

Libby settled at a table and showed her the photo, holding out little hope, but the blonde licked cream from her fingers, screwed up her nose in thought, and announced she had a friend who sometimes worked on a training farm. 'They have lots of different dogs. Shetlands, Old English sheepdogs, you name it. Some of them had a funny name – like carpet.'

Libby could hardly believe her luck. 'Carpathian?'

'That's it.'

'Do you have an address?'

'For my friend?'

Libby was patient. 'No, for the training place.'

'Oh.' The girl looked blank. 'Miles away. What was it? Something farm.'

Libby waited.

'I know. Johnson's. Or was it Jenson's. Yes, that was it. Like the racing driver, you know?'

A woman peered round the door to the kitchens. 'Ready to serve the customer, Maria?'

'Yes, s'pose so.' Maria looked less than enthusiastic as Libby ordered coffee. 'Jenson's Farm. Thanks for your help.'

The woman came further into the room, frowning. 'Mind if I ask why you want that place?'

'I heard about their dogs.'

'Press, are you? Journalist? I don't like the press. Intruding on people. You leave them alone. They're new here, trying to make a living, setting up a sheepdog training business on their farm. No money in sheep alone, these days.'

'No, it's not that. I mean, I'm not from the newspapers. I – we have a dog. Like the ones they train.' Libby tried to get a grip. 'I mean, we've lost our dog and I wondered if they could help.'

'You're with that man, then.'

'A man?' Hope flickered in Libby's heart.

'Tall, grey hair. Nice blue eyes. Said something about a dog gone missing.'

Libby was following in Max's footsteps. That meant she was on the right track. 'Yes. He's my – well, it's our dog.'

'Then, I'll show you on the map, like I showed him when he came this way yesterday.' She drew roads on the back of a menu. 'There you are: Jenson's Farm. Quiet folk. Keep to themselves. Been tenants on the farm for a couple of years, but making a decent fist of it. Took one of their dogs to the local show, came second in their class, working the sheep.'

Grateful, Libby took the hastily scrawled map, gulped a cup of watery coffee, and set off for Jenson's Farm, looking forward to finding Max and talking to the sheepdog trainers.

* * *

Following the map, Libby came upon a sign heralding Jenson's farm. She turned the corner and slammed on the brake as she caught sight of a familiar vehicle. Max's car was half hidden in a small patch of woodland beside the farm lane. Libby turned her car until it was parallel with the Land Rover and climbed out.

The Land Rover was deserted. Squinting, she looked around, but there was no sign of Max or Shipley. Puzzled, she locked the Citroen and set off up the road leading to the farm. She'd hardly gone twenty yards when a loud hiss made her jump.

'Libby.' To her delight, it was Max's voice. 'Over here.'

'Where? I can't see you.'

'To your left.'

Libby slipped into a small copse of trees. There was Max, Shipley sitting obediently by his side. Libby hardly knew whether she was more impressed by Shipley's improved behaviour, or perturbed by Max's secrecy. 'What on earth is going on?' Max, dressed in a dark jacket and black jeans, wore a black beanie on his head. 'And why are you wearing that ridiculous hat? It's not in the least bit cold today.'

Max's beam split his face in two. 'I'm hiding – staking out the farmhouse. I've spent a couple of days talking to local people, gathering information, and I reckon Bear's likely to be here.'

For a second, Libby's heart leapt. Then, reason kicked in. 'This farm's legitimate, I believe. They're openly training dogs. I've just come from a café in Hereford, and they told me everyone knows. It's all above board. I was on my way to visit.'

'Ah, but where do they get the dogs? That's the point. There's at least half a dozen there, various breeds. If we go marching up to the farmhouse looking for a missing animal they'll know we're suspicious. I'm waiting for it to get dark and I'm going to investigate.'

'Aren't you jumping to conclusions?'

Max shook his head. 'I called at another farm, nearby. They told me this was a busy place with vans constantly arriving and leaving. That farmer was an old timer. He said he'd been suspicious about sheep rustling, as there's been a spate of that recently, but when he heard they were training dogs, he stopped worrying.'

'How do we know they're stealing the dogs?' Libby objected.

'We don't, but I'm going to give Shipley a chance to prove his worth. I put one of Bear's blankets in the Land Rover. It's full of dried dribble. I'm going to see if Shipley can pick up Bear's trail. Call it a test of his new skills.'

Libby looked up at the sky. 'It's going to be ages until it gets dark. What if someone drives past and sees the cars?'

'I've been here a few hours, now. Several cars have driven in and out and none of them noticed me.'

'What are we going to do from now until sunset?'

'What's this about we?' Max had his hands on his hips. 'I'm staying here with Shipley. You need to go home and let me get on with it.'

'And miss all the fun? You must be joking. You're not getting rid of me that easily.'

Max looked as though he'd like to argue, but after a moment, he shrugged. 'In that case let's get into the Land Rover. I brought plenty of provisions with me.'

They walked back to the cars. 'We need to move your car farther into the trees,' Max remarked. 'If you're going to join me on spying expeditions in future, you may want to rethink your vehicle. This purple affair's a little too visible for my liking.'

Libby scratched her head. 'Maybe we could cover it with branches?'

Max chuckled. 'You've been watching too many television programmes. This isn't World War II, you know. We'll just put your car behind mine for safety. You'll need to manoeuvre between the trees, but at least your ancient and battered vehicle is small.'

'And, of course, I'm a brilliant driver. Don't forget that.'

The cars out of sight, they settled comfortably in the Land Rover. 'Good job it's not midwinter,' Max pointed out. 'We can't use the engine, in case it draws attention to us, so there's no heating. If you're cold there's another rug here.' Libby turned towards the back seat. Max grabbed her arm. 'Not that one, that's Bear's.'

'I need food.' Libby was suddenly ravenous. 'What have you brought?'

'Some of your very own sausage rolls from my freezer, and some pies I bought in Hereford. Not especially healthy, I'm afraid, but it will fill us up.'

'The diet's on hold, then?'

While they ate, Shipley lying comfortably behind them, Libby filled Max in on progress in the search for Beryl's killer. 'I'm confused about William and Margery,' she confessed. 'His heart attack was genuine enough. I suspect Margery has quite a tongue on her, and if she accused him of adultery, I'm not surprised he became agitated. But, it rules him out from the attack on his wife. He was already in hospital when it happened.'

Max tapped a finger on the steering wheel. 'I see what you mean. Unless he hired someone to take out his wife.'

'Come on, Max. That's going a bit far.' She didn't admit to having had the same thought herself.

'Can't rule it out, though. Did his wife recognise her attacker?'

'She says not.'

'And do you believe her?'

Libby considered, her head on one side. 'Not sure, to be honest. Their relationship is pretty complicated.'

Max laughed. 'I don't know of any relationship that isn't, especially if they've been married for forty odd years. A lot can happen in that time.'

'So, we won't cross William off the list of suspects yet.'

'Who else could be involved?'

'Almost anyone,' Libby sighed, 'who's ever been inside Beryl's house.'

'Most people in Exham, then. Other society members, maybe? If it's one of them, it rules out a crime of passion. Everyone in the society's at least middle-aged – not that over forties can't be passionate, but you know what I mean. They're not hormonal teenagers carrying knives in their back pockets.'

'Actually, there are a couple of new recruits. Annabel Pearson is around your cut-off date of forty, I would think, but Joanna, the doctor's wife, is even younger. She let slip that Beryl wasn't the sweet little old lady she appeared to be, and Mandy heard gossip that confirmed it. There's something about shady dealings, involving using clients' money, quite apart from the drinking problem. That's why she left her job in the spring.'

Max was nodding. 'Sounds like there's still plenty of work to be done. Let's find Bear and then we can get back to it.'

'There's another thing.' Libby told him about Terence Marchant's new shop, due to open in two weeks time. 'Angela's setting up the biggest party Exham has ever seen. We're going to get everyone into the shop for a wine and chocolate party that will scare off Terence Marchant and his posh French pastries, before he even begins. Angela has some sort of secret up her sleeve. She won't tell me about it.'

Max looked at his watch. 'If you've had enough to eat, I suggest you settle down and catch forty winks while you can. It'll be dark soon and then the fun will start.'

Libby yawned. It was true, she did feel drowsy. It was good to be with Max again. She could relax for a while.

19

BISCUIT CRUMBS

It seemed she'd only been asleep for five minutes when Max shook her awake, but the light had gone. The trees around the car had become sinister shapes in the gloom. 'Come on, time to go sleuthing.' Max's voice resonated with excitement.

Once out of the car, he held Bear's blanket close to Shipley's nose. The dog wagged his tail and sniffed the ground, but made no sign of finding his old friend's trail. 'They'll have been keeping Bear hidden on the farm, and he would have arrived in some kind of vehicle. We need to get nearer before Shipley will pick up the scent.'

In the dark, Libby kept close to Max, sliding between the trees that led up to the house as he lit a narrow path with his torch. Shipley kept his nose to the ground, tail wagging. 'He was born for this sort of work,' Max murmured.

'I think all his over-excitement happens when he's bored,' Libby whispered.

Max touched her arm. 'Don't whisper. Talk in a deep voice. Whispers carry for miles.'

'I said, he was bored,' Libby intoned, in the deepest voice she could manage, making Max shake with helpless laughter.

Regaining self-control, he waved his hand under Libby's nose, and they trod towards a group of sheds to the right of the farmhouse. 'Are you sure there's no one in there?'

'I can't be certain. While I've been watching the place, everyone who arrived, also left.'

Max stopped and held up a finger. 'What's that?'

Libby listened. 'It's a dog. Dogs. Lots of them. They're here.' She watched Shipley, who was still working, zigzagging with his nose to the ground, but showing no sign of excitement. 'We need to know if Bear's here. If not, the place could be legitimate. You did give Shipley a good sniff at Bear's blanket, didn't you?'

'If Bear's nearby, I'm confident he'll pick up the scent.'

Out in the Herefordshire countryside, there were no street lamps. The moon was a crescent shaped sliver high in the sky, providing the faintest of light. It was easy to slip round the side of the barn keeping the building between themselves and the farmhouse, just in case they were mistaken and the owners were still at home.

Shipley had shown no sign of sensing Bear until they were close to the building. Suddenly, his head went up and he stopped dead, shaking with excitement, tail wagging madly. Libby gasped. 'He's here. Shipley can smell him. You were right to suspect this place.'

'This way,' said Max. 'I can see the door on the other side.' Gently he pushed the door, but nothing happened. 'It's locked.' He reached into a pocket. 'I'm so glad. I've been wanting to use this kit for a long time.' He jangled a handful of metal.

'What's that?'

'A set of burglars' skeleton keys. Give me a minute, and I'll have this lock open.'

Libby waited patiently as he fiddled with it. Her feet grew cold. 'How are you getting on?'

'Not as easy as I hoped,' he admitted. 'I've practised at home, but it's more difficult in the dark. Wait, I think I've got it.' Max shoved at the door, but the lock held. He swore.

'Let me have a go.' Libby took the keys from him, inserted one into the lock, and jiggled it. For a long moment, nothing happened, then the lock clicked open.

'I loosened it for you,' Max muttered.

He pulled the door open and slipped inside, Libby following with Shipley at her side.

An acrid smell of dogs, urine, and meat made Libby blink. The barn held at least twenty animals, each in a tiny pen equipped with a bowl of water and another dish, presumably for food. Most of the containers near Libby were empty, or held a few biscuit crumbs. 'This place is a disgrace,' she whispered.

'Be quick. Find Bear,' Max commanded, but Shipley stood close to the door, making no attempt to move. 'Come on, Shipley,' Max said. 'Don't tell me you can't find Bear in here.'

Libby searched the pens. As she passed each one, the dog inside whined and ran to the barrier, hopeful she would offer food. With every step, her heart fell further. 'He's not here.'

'He must be. Maybe he's asleep.'

'Look.' She pointed at Shipley. 'He's telling us Bear's not here.'

Her spirits were in her boots. 'We were wrong,' she groaned. 'There's every breed of dog here, but no Bear. What do we do now?'

'We'll get back to the car and go home with our tails between our legs.' Max's voice was flat with disappointment. 'In the morning, I'll talk to the police. We don't even know for sure if these dogs are stolen, but they're neglected and the police will investigate properly.' He kicked angrily at a railing. 'I'm sure Bear's been here. Shipley could smell him.'

Libby shared his anger at the plight of the dogs. 'No one should keep fully grown dogs in such tiny spaces, with nothing to eat or drink. Besides, if they're stolen, they all have fond owners, waiting at home—'

Shipley interrupted with a low growl. He stood at the door, his nose pointing back along the track that led to the farm. Libby followed him and looked out, just as a car swerved around the corner, headlights lighting up the farm buildings. She blinked in the glare and, suddenly scared, pulled Shipley to the side, away from the door. She dropped a warning hand on his head and held her breath, hoping the dog would remain silent.

'Max,' she hissed. 'Someone's coming.'

Max flicked off his torch. The door rattled and the dogs in the barn set up a cacophony of hysterical barking. Libby and Max froze, their backs against the wall, Libby praying no one would enter. To her dismay, a tall man with a bucket in one hand kicked the door wide open and walked in. 'No need for all that racket,' he shouted as the barking intensified. 'Quit your whining.'

He shoved open the gate to one of the pens and aimed a kick at the dog inside, a silky coated collie. Libby bit back a cry. He hadn't caught sight of her or Max in the gloom, and he walked between the pens, tossing lumps of meat over the railings, some falling in the dogs' dishes, some dropping randomly onto the dirty straw of the pens. Max touched Libby's elbow. Quietly, as the man reached the far end of the barn, they tiptoed to the door.

For a moment, Libby thought they'd made it, but just as Max had his hand on the door, the new arrival swung round, dropped the bucket, and shouted, 'Oy. You there. Stop where you are.'

Max and Libby ran outside, closely followed by Shipley, as the man bellowed, 'Scott! Get 'em!'

His companion stood by the car, scrabbling in the boot. At the sound of his accomplice's voice he turned and raised his arms. He had a shotgun.

Libby bit back a scream and ran, as a shot rang out and whistled past her head.

The man from the shed shouted, 'Get in the car, Scott. Run 'em down.'

He'd reckoned without Shipley.

Like lightning, the dog raced at Scott, leaped in the air with wide-open jaws and clamped his teeth tightly onto the man's arm.

'Get off me,' his prisoner screamed, struggling, but Shipley hung on, shaken from side to side, growling deep in his throat. The villain's gun flew out of his grasp.

His companion took one look, turned, and ran. He wasn't going anywhere near the wild dog.

'Get back to the car,' Max ordered, and gave Libby a push in the direction of the woods. She shook off his arm. She wasn't about to leave Shipley to the attention of those men.

Furious, she ran across, grabbed the gun and sprinted after Scott's accomplice.

Too late, the man heard her approach, spun round, and aimed a blow at her head, but she ducked, the blow missed, and with all her strength, she swung the gun. With a dull clunk, it thudded into the man's body.

He screamed, clutched his shoulder and fell. Libby kept the gun trained on him, holding it against her shoulder, hoping against hope she wouldn't need to fire it. She'd never fired any kind of gun.

Max shouted, 'Let him go, Shipley,' and to Libby's astonishment, the dog released Scott's arm and stood guard, still growling.

Max gestured to Scott. 'You'd better sit next to your friend.'

Scott screamed, furious. 'Your dog's broke my arm. I'll have the law on—' He stopped as Max talked into his phone.

'Quite.' Max smiled. 'The law is on its way.'

Libby nodded. 'So, let's just wait patiently until they arrive.'

* * *

'Now, that was fun.' Max's cheeks glowed. A couple of bemused police officers had driven off with the dog thieves in tow, with promises to Libby that they'd call the RSPCA to look after the dogs. Libby, Max, and Shipley were on the road back to Exham, Libby's car left hidden in the trees. They'd collect it tomorrow. For now, they wanted to be together.

Libby's hands hadn't stopped shaking. 'I'm not cut out for this sort of thing,' she admitted.

'Well, you insisted on coming along.' Max took one hand from the wheel and hugged her. 'Apart from beating that man with the gun, you're a natural with skeleton keys. Are you sure you weren't a burglar in your former life?'

Shipley barked from the back of the Land Rover. Libby leaned back to scratch his head. 'You were wonderful, Shipley.'

Max chuckled. 'Good thing I had you with me. I think I may be getting a bit old. My knees will punish me, tomorrow. I'll leave the fighting to you, in future.'

Libby's glow of achievement faded as the adrenaline wore off. 'The trouble is,' she said. 'We're no nearer to finding Bear. I was so sure he'd be there.'

'Me too. I'm sorry.'

Libby blew her nose, reaction setting in. 'What are we going to do?'

'For the moment, we'll go home, and then we'll start again.'

She looked out into the darkness. 'Poor Bear. He's out there, somewhere, all alone. He'll be so lonely.'

'Bear can cope.' But Max's voice was uncertain.

'I hope you're right.' The thought of her beloved animal, possibly in another dirty shed, short of food, and wondering if he'd been abandoned forever, was too much for Libby. 'If we find him, I won't ever let him out of my sight,' she wailed.

Max changed gear. 'Not if – when we find him. We won't give up, will we, Shipley?' In the back of the car, the spaniel gave a short, sharp bark, as if in agreement.

20

WINE AND CHOCOLATE

On the morning of the Brown's Bakery party, Libby planned to spend the rest of the day quietly. She visited Angela to check the arrangements and gossip about her adventures in Hereford, basking for a while in her friend's open-mouthed admiration. 'You mean, you whacked him yourself? With a gun? Good for you!'

Libby confessed she'd been shaking for hours afterwards. 'But the worst is, we're no farther forward.'

'Think about the animals you saved. Their owners will be thrilled.'

'I'd feel better if we had a starting point, but the Hereford farm was our only lead,' she confided. 'The thieves must have sold him off before we arrived.' With an effort, she changed the subject. 'Anyway, I didn't come here to moan. How are the preparations for our party going?'

Angela waved a file of notes. 'It's all in hand, and there's an extra item; a wine tasting.'

'Really? Who's going to run it? I can't think of anyone in Exham, now the off licence is closed.'

Angela grinned. 'Well, you'll see.'

Libby gave her friend a long look. 'You're looking bright eyed and bushy tailed, today. Has something good happened?'

Her friend's burst of giggles gave Libby a clue. Angela never giggled. 'It's that man, isn't it?'

'He's coming to the party, so you'll meet him.'

Libby hugged her friend. 'Come on, tell me everything.'

'He's the same age as me, and a widower. He's in the restaurant business, which is how we met. I had lunch with my nephew in London, in one of Owen's restaurants, and Steve knocked over the wine bottle. Owen sent one of waiters to help and gave us another table. Things went on from there.'

'I can't wait to meet him.' The penny dropped. 'Is he going to run the wine tasting?'

Angela beamed. 'He is, he's giving his services free and he's supplying the wine at cost.'

Libby's jaw dropped. 'That's so generous.'

'And that's not all...'

'What do you mean?'

Angela was hugging her arms with glee. 'You'll have to wait until tonight. Anyway, that's enough about me. How's the Beryl investigation going?'

'Slowly.' Libby groaned. 'I feel as though I'm going in circles. She didn't seem to have any enemies, just a bunch of supportive friends, any of whom could easily have poisoned her whisky. The police have cleared the students, at least, because none of them knew her and they weren't anywhere near her at the castle. All we're left with is her alcohol problem.' She paused. 'I have one thought about that...'

'Go on,' Angela pleaded.

'Not yet. It's just an idea. Tell me, what do you notice happens when people drink too much?'

Her friend thought for a moment. 'They get talkative, and then miserable and maudlin, and then they fall asleep.'

'That's exactly right.'

'How does that help find Beryl's killer?'

'Wait until this evening. I have an idea, and it's going to be quite a night.'

* * *

The Exham on Sea Community Centre had never looked so cheerful. After hours of heart searching, and in consultation with Frank, Angela had suggested moving the party away from the bakery, because it seemed everyone in town wanted to be there. Libby was bemused. 'How have you persuaded people to stump up for a ticket?'

Angela winked. 'The tickets include a glass of wine and snacks, and everyone will get a few free chocolates. Frank's agreed it's about building support, rather than making a profit. He'll be happy if we just break even, and the goodwill should last a long time.'

'I hope you're right. Terence Marchant's patisserie will be a novelty, and I'm worried people won't be able to resist his mille-feuilles and macarons. Still,' determined not to be a misery, Libby stuck out her chin, 'there's plenty of custom for everyone.'

She hoped the wine would loosen tongues, and the unspoken Exham habit of keeping secrets might be overcome. She had a mental list of people she intended to question.

Mandy climbed a step-ladder, holding the last garland. She was upbeat. 'At least Terence Marchant's not going to sell chocolates.'

'You're right. Let's enjoy the evening. It's a good opportunity for a celebration, anyway.'

Angela giggled. 'We can always use one of those, and you need cheering up, Libby.' Her cheeks were suddenly suffused with colour. Libby followed her gaze to the door. A short, round man had arrived. He wore John Lennon spectacles and a beaming smile.

As he advanced up the room, Libby looked from him to Angela. The expression on Angela's face, her eyes warm with pleasure as she watched him arrive, told Libby all she needed to know. This wasn't at all how she'd expected elegant Angela's new man to look, but there was no doubting her friend's happiness.

'Libby,' Angela said. 'This is Owen. He's going to run the wine tasting for us.'

Owen's smile spread endearingly across his face, almost stretching from ear to ear. 'I've heard all about you and your exploits, and I'm honoured to meet you. Angela's set me quite a task, matching wine and chocolate, but I hope you'll enjoy the result.'

Max's arrival at that moment, accompanied by Shipley, gave Libby a chance to recover her equilibrium. She liked Angela's man already.

Shipley lay down on command, only a twitching tail hinting that he was on full alert. Angela seemed mesmerised. 'I can't believe it's the same dog. I've never seen him so quiet.'

Max grinned. 'He's had some serious training, and I've brought him along this evening to prove he can behave properly when the room's full of people.'

Libby placed a bowl of water in one corner. 'There you are, Shipley. I'm glad you're here.' She loved the newly trained spaniel, but he was no replacement for Bear. Libby's last hope was Gemma Humberstone. The detective constable, maintaining their delicate truce, had promised to come to the party. She'd sat in with a colleague from West Mercia as he interviewed the owners of the farm, and with any luck, she'd have news.

'Balloons.' Mandy cut into Libby's thoughts. 'We need more, Mrs F. Get puffing, people.'

Libby discovered it was impossible to stay sad while blowing up balloons. Angela agreed. 'It's like singing. Something about using your lungs properly.'

At that, Mandy blew too hard and the balloon burst, with an explosion that would have sent the unreconstructed Shipley into a spin. This time, he barely moved. Max beamed, as though he'd undertaken the animal's training himself. 'Look at that reformed character.'

Libby glanced at her watch. 'Hurry up, it's almost time to open the doors. Angela, will you collect tickets while Mandy and I set out the chocolates? Max, you're in charge of making sure Shipley doesn't steal any.' Within moments, the room buzzed. Songs from the West Country's favourite rural band, The Wurzels, played through a loudspeaker in the intervals between Owen's observations on wine. Local people sat at gingham-covered tables, ate, drank, and sang along.

Libby manned the counter at the end of the room, selling Mrs Forest's Chocolates, and as the noise level rose and the wine levels fell, she secured dozens of orders.

Mandy took over at last, and Libby slipped away to join the history society, who'd commandeered a large round table in a corner. She squeezed in next to Joanna, who'd already drained one glass of wine and was half way down another. 'Quite an occasion, Mrs Forest. You must be thrilled.'

Libby placed a bowl of chocolates in the centre of the table. 'Help yourself,' she encouraged. Joanna did not need to be told twice. As she leaned forward, selected a chocolate in the shape of a champagne bottle, and popped it in her mouth, Libby asked, 'How are you settling in? I hope people are friendly.'

'Oh yes. Everyone's been most kind, and I make a point of visiting some of the older folk.'

'That's wonderful. I'm sure they appreciate it.'

'Mrs Halfstead, for instance.' Joanna's eyes were bright, and she seemed eager to talk. 'I popped in this morning, just to see how she is. It must be terrible, with her husband under suspicion for this dreadful murder, and then, someone tried to kill her. She seemed very calm.' Joanna leaned closer to Libby. 'A bit too calm, maybe? I did wonder, you know—' She cleared her throat and continued in a whisper, 'I wondered if some of her story might have been made up.'

'Well, she was definitely stabbed.'

'Yes, but not very hard. I mean, no real damage done. Maybe,' her voice was an almost inaudible hiss, 'maybe she and William were in it together.' Triumphant, Joanna nodded and took a long swig of wine.

Libby asked. 'What makes you think that?'

'Well, who knows what goes on within a marriage? I know I would always stand up for Jeremy, whatever he did, but not all wives are as patient as I am.' Her lip quivered a little. Perhaps her marriage to the doctor was not as perfect as she wanted Libby to believe. 'Anyway, I heard William left his teaching job, and then, there was that business with Beryl's drinking and the accounts.' She gave a little tinkling laugh that jangled on Libby's nerves. 'Maybe William and Beryl were in cahoots and Margery found out about it. If William had killed once, he might have become overconfident and had a shot at getting rid of his wife.'

'It's a theory,' Libby said. 'But it couldn't be William who stabbed his wife, because he was already in hospital.'

Joanna's face fell. 'So, he was. I'll have to leave the sleuthing to you, Mrs Forest. Come on, do tell me what you think. It's so exciting, isn't it, to have a real-life mystery to solve?'

'Well, I don't know much more than you, I'm afraid. Have another chocolate.'

Joanna took a chocolate, swallowed it, and stared into her glass. 'Oh, dear, this is finished. I'll just get a top-up. Can I get one for you?'

Libby shook her head. 'No thanks.'

She moved to sit between George Edwards and Mrs Moffat. George watched Joanna as she staggered a little. His voice was harsh. 'That young lady's a bit too fond of the bottle, if you ask me. You can't trust a woman who drinks too much, no matter how long you've known them.'

Mrs Moffat said, 'I don't think everything is as it should be at the doctor's house. I saw him lunching with the receptionist the other day, in Exham, and they seemed to be getting on awfully well.' She raised her eyebrows. 'If you know what I mean.'

Libby managed a polite smile and turned to George. 'Is your wife not well today?'

He sighed. 'No, another difficult day, I'm afraid. I'm about to go home – I promised to buy some chocolates. Deirdre likes the ones with coconut. I can't manage them. The coconut gets under my plate.' Libby started, confused, before realising he was talking about false teeth. She tried hard not to stare.

He was still talking. 'I'll be buying plenty of boxes. I'm going fishing early tomorrow and I always give Deirdre a little present on fishing days. She doesn't like me going, not since that business at the club, but I tell her, people can think what they like, I won those trophies, fair and square.'

His face flushed an unhealthy shade of dark red. 'How dare they accuse me of cheating.' He banged his fist on the table, then seemed to collect himself, the flash of temper over, 'Before I go, I like to take her breakfast in bed.'

Max had arrived in time to hear the last few words. 'There, Libby. Married life means breakfast in bed.'

'Every day?'

'Well, let's just say, sometimes. But I came to get you. Gemma Humberstone just arrived, and she's bursting to tell us something.' He added, 'I'm sorry to say, Ian Smith's here as well.'

Libby leapt to her feet, paying no attention to Ian Smith, who was making a bee-line for the stacks of chocolates for sale. She wanted to hear what Gemma had discovered. 'Has she found Bear?'

Max took her hand. 'Not yet, I'm afraid, but she has news.'

Gemma looked young and pretty, and several male heads turned her way. 'The workers at the farm don't own the place, and they were only too willing to talk to me. I think they're hoping to get credit in court for grassing up the man behind the thefts. They say their only job is to look after the dogs. They know nothing about where the animals come from.'

Max snorted. 'A likely story.'

Libby, heart racing, interrupted. 'Did they know anything about Bear?'

Gemma grinned. 'They said two Carpathian sheepdogs arrived at the farm a few days ago, but they travelled on the next day. At first, they denied knowing where the dogs went, but eventually they gave us some addresses. There aren't many animals like Bear in the country, so he'd fetch a decent price.'

'And it should be easy to find him?'

Libby's spirits rose, but Gemma grimaced. 'Unfortunately, Bear was a bit too clever for the thieves. They loaded him into the van but they didn't lock the doors. After they'd been on the road a while, they stopped at a service station, leaving the dogs alone in the van. Half an hour later, when the thieves returned to the vehicle, the doors were open and Bear and a couple of other animals had disappeared.'

Max raised his glass. 'Good for you, Bear.'

Libby groaned. 'But, that means he's wandering around somewhere. Lost. Where was the van?'

'Just this side of Worcester. One of our officers is on his way to speak to the prospective owners. We may have a case against them, if they know the dogs they're buying have been stolen.'

'That's all very well,' Libby wailed, 'but what about Bear? He's lost, and the nights are drawing in. Anything could happen to him, and we're no nearer finding him than we were before.'

She looked around the room. Everyone was having such a fun time, but all she wanted to do was get away. She'd hoped to unmask Beryl's murderer, and her suspicions had increased during the evening, but there was one more item of evidence she wanted to check. 'Max, I'm going to go home early. Angela and her new man have everything under control, here.'

'I'll come with you.' Max's concern was touching.

'No, I'm fine. I'll feel better if you're here to help Angela lock up.'

Max hesitated before agreeing. 'If that's what you want. I'll come over when this is all done. Cheer up. The evening's been an enormous success. If this doesn't scare Terence Marchant away, nothing will—'

A shriek broke in to the conversation. At the other end of the room, Mandy, fists clenched, was facing down Ian Smith, her face incandescent with fury.

'All right, all right. No need to make a fuss. I didn't mean any harm...' Smith backed away, hands in the air.

Someone nearby applauded. 'Good for you, Mandy.' Libby saw an open box of chocolates, lying half empty on the floor. She stared at Ian Smith. A chocolate cream had lodged, squashed and oozing, behind his ear.

'What happened?'

Mandy, red-faced with fury, pointed at the hapless figure. 'He pinched my bottom.'

'I did not,' Ian Smith blustered. 'I just gave you a little pat on the behind. Friendly, that was all. No need to throw things, silly little—'

'You'd better get out of here, Smith,' Max broke in. 'You're not welcome.'

'But I didn't do anything.'

As Mandy grabbed another box of chocolates and took a step forward, the PC shrugged. 'All right, I'm going,' he muttered. 'Can't take a joke, that's the trouble with you Goths. I could have you for assaulting a policeman.'

Gemma was close behind. 'Mandy, do you want to press charges? I'm sure there are plenty of witnesses here.'

Mandy shrugged. 'I'll think about it.'

21

STEAK

Libby's head pounded as she arrived at the cottage. Ian Smith's behaviour had been the last straw. She opened the back door and called for Bear, as she'd done every time she returned home since his disappearance. There was no sign of him. She must learn to accept he was gone.

Aspirin, that was what she needed for this headache. She opened the cabinet in the kitchen, where she kept a first aid kit and a small supply of medicines, and sorted through the contents. She found the aspirin, and some vitamins she never remembered to take. She turned on the tap to fill a glass with water.

What was that?

She held her breath and listened. Another dull thud sounded from above.

She called up the stairs, 'Fuzzy, what are you doing? If you're winding wool everywhere...' The cat sometimes played with the balls of wool from a basket in the upstairs study. Libby was an incompetent knitter, too impatient to take the time to enjoy the activity, so her basket was full of half-finished scarves and hats.

She'd once come home to find green double knitting wool wrapped tightly around her chair and desk.

She climbed the stairs, calling the cat's name, and found Fuzzy in the airing cupboard. 'Stopped you just in time, didn't I? It's no good trying to look innocent.'

Fuzzy stretched, scratched a towel into a heap, turned round three times, and settled down to sleep.

Libby entered her study. The information she needed was in her files. She was sure Margery had told her something vital.

She grasped the handle of the top drawer of her filing cabinet, and it slid open. 'That's odd. I thought it was locked.' She shrugged, pulled out all her notes from Beryl's case, and started to read, muttering as though Fuzzy was listening, 'I can't see anything odd after all, except for that person Margery saw. She thought it was a volunteer, someone she didn't know. The police never did discover who it was.'

She re-read the description and gasped, her heart racing.

She snatched up a different notebook, the one containing her notes from the history society meeting. 'That's it. I knew it...'

The words died in her mouth. 'What's that?' she cried out. The thud had come from her bedroom, and it wasn't Fuzzy.

Libby swallowed. 'Is there someone there?'

No reply.

Trying not to breathe, Libby got to her feet and took a step towards the open door. She leaned back, eyes fixed on the corridor, fingers walking across the desk until they tapped against the heavy lighthouse statue she used as a paperweight. She grasped it, hand damp with sweat, and licked her lips.

A shuffling sound came from the bedroom. There was someone there, and Libby was in no mood to run. She'd dealt with the dog thieves. She could deal with her burglar, especially if it was the person she suspected of killing Beryl.

She closed her eyes briefly, took a breath and strode out of the study. With two quick steps she was at her bedroom door. She flung it open, just as the louvred door of the wardrobe clicked shut.

'Come out, whoever you are.'

No one answered. Had she imagined it? No. She could hear breathing from the wardrobe.

With a jolt, Libby came to her senses. She was alone with only a paperweight as a weapon, and if her suspicions were correct, the person in hiding there had already killed once. She needed to get out of the house and phone for help. Slowly, she backed out of the room. 'I'm leaving,' she announced, trying to sound firm.

As she reached the door, she turned to run. The wardrobe door flew open as she spun round, the paperweight held aloft, and faced the most genial member of the history society, Beryl's lifelong friend, George Edwards.

'You shouldn't have come back.' He murmured. 'I didn't want to hurt you, but it's your own fault, Libby.' He took a step forward.

Libby edged back, out of the bedroom door. She stammered, 'I know you killed Beryl.'

He whimpered, 'I couldn't trust her any more. She was my oldest friend, the only person who ever guessed my secret. She promised she'd keep it safe, but she was drinking too much. Her tongue kept running away with her.' His eyes pleaded for understanding. 'I couldn't let her tell Deirdre about me. It would kill my wife.'

He took a step closer. 'How did you know?'

Libby backed away, judging the distance to the stairs with a glance. A memory flashed into her head of George's wife, lying back on a chair, shaking her head, the hair of her wig remaining perfectly groomed. 'At the society meeting, I realised Deirdre wore a wig. Then, Margery described both the woman she saw at the castle and the woman who attacked her. The descriptions matched so closely it had to be the same person.'

Deirdre was housebound and too fragile to be the killer, but George had easy access to his wife's wigs and bright clothes.

The solution had seemed crazy at first, but the facts fitted together, and Libby had remembered Joe's advice to follow where the evidence led. She looked George in the eye. 'You like to dress in women's clothes, don't you?'

If she could keep him talking, she could reach the stairs and get away. 'What did Beryl know?'

George's face worked as tears filled his eyes. 'About me? Everything. I had to tell someone, and she was my oldest friend. I trusted her, and she kept the secret for years, but after she lost her job, she was drinking more and more. I knew she'd give me away, one day.'

Libby took another step backwards.

George's face twisted. 'It started with Deirdre's dresses, soon after we married. I used to try them on when she went out. Then, it was her – her underwear. She never knew. After her first dose of chemotherapy, years ago, she lost her hair and bought a couple of wigs.'

His face crumbled into self-pity. 'You wouldn't understand, but wearing her clothes, dressing as a woman, made me feel true to myself, for the first time in my life.' His eyes gleamed at the memory, and Libby felt a pang of sympathy. He'd had to hide his real feelings for so many years.

'I often visited the castle. I felt safe there. The building was big enough for me to avoid anyone I knew. I could wear Deirdre's clothes, and lipstick.'

He chuckled, suddenly, and Libby's compassion drained away. 'I planned it all. I bet you didn't know how easy it is to extract nicotine. Just like making tea, but with cigarettes instead of teabags!'

His smug expression was sickening. He was boasting, now, following Libby as she inched towards the stairs. 'I visited Beryl one evening, and when she left the room, I put poison in her silver flask. Silly woman,' he sneered. 'She thought no one knew about that flask. She'd told me she was playing the maid next day. So proud, she was. Full of herself.'

His eyes narrowed to angry slits. 'I should have stayed away, but I couldn't resist seeing if my plan worked. Then, Margery Halfstead saw me. She didn't recognise me, but I couldn't take the risk.'

He shrugged. 'I went to the house to kill her, but I couldn't bring myself to do it. Not with a knife. It was easy enough to put poison in Beryl's whisky, though. No blood, you see. I read how to make the poison on the internet.' His voice had become conversational, as though he was chatting with Libby about the weather. She glanced behind. She was at the top of the stairs.

'Stop.' George's face changed. 'I can't let you go, now.' His eyes glittered. He raised his hands, fingers curled, and lunged.

Libby was younger than he, and faster. She fled down the stairs, running for her life, a scream in her throat.

George was almost on her. Terrified, she looked back and tripped, falling heavily.

With a growl that shook the walls, Bear jumped over Libby and leapt at George.

* * *

Suddenly, the house was full. Max grabbed George and held him on the floor, as Shipley brought up the rear, barking wildly.

Flanked by the dogs, their eyes following George's every

move, Max sat on the killer's chest as Libby phoned for the police. George had visibly shrivelled. He looked old and pathetic. 'I knew it would come out, one day, but I couldn't face everyone knowing.' His face crumpled, he dropped his head into his hands, shoulders shaking with sobs, and muttered, 'I never wanted to kill Beryl, but she knew about me. I couldn't trust her...' The rest of the sentence was lost in sobs.

Revulsion rose in Libby's throat. 'You murdered one woman and tried to kill another, just to hide your weakness from your wife. How could you?'

Max looked from one to the other, puzzled, but before Libby could fill in the details, the police arrived.

Libby gave a short statement to a wide-eyed Gemma Humberstone, and, too tired to talk more that evening, agreed to go to the police station early the next day to give all the details. Meanwhile, another officer marched George to the car.

At last, Libby and Max were alone with their dogs.

Libby sat on the floor, her arm round the giant sheepdog. 'Where did Bear come from, at exactly the right moment?'

'One of my old mates, Alan Jenkins at the garage, saw Bear wandering through the lanes on his way home. He must have walked about twenty miles a day. Alan knew about your party, and brought Bear along, but they arrived about ten minutes after you left. I was going to ring you, but then I thought we'd come to the cottage and surprise you.'

'It's just as well you did, although I think I'm probably stronger than George. I could have beaten him off.' Libby tried not to recall the sheer panic she'd felt, as she fled down the stairs. She shivered. 'Imagine. Mild mannered George Edwards. What a mess he's made of his life.'

Max squatted, examining Bear's body with gentle hands. 'He

seems all right. His feet are sore, of course, but other than that, he looks pretty sprightly.'

'No wonder he's filthy, and thin, poor animal.' Bear lay with his head in Libby's lap, panting, as she talked. 'I suppose he hasn't had a square meal since he escaped from the van. I'll get him some food.' She staggered to her feet. 'You too, Shipley. You've both been wonderful.'

'We'll take him to the vet, tomorrow, but I think he's just tired. Come on, Bear, you'll sleep well tonight.' Max followed them to the kitchen. 'I'm not sure I understand why George broke into your house. He didn't come to kill you, did he?'

'No. He hadn't brought his knife. He'd come to raid my filing cabinet, to see what I'd found out, I suppose. I had planned to unmask him at the party. I was pretty sure he was the killer, once I realised Margery's attacker, and the unknown person in the castle, wore a wig like Deirdre's.'

She attempted a smile. 'I was planning a little drama, but when Gemma told me Bear was lost again, I couldn't bring myself to do it. I made an excuse to myself, that I needed to check Margery's evidence first.' She shivered. 'I was at George's table earlier in the evening, when he talked about women who drink too much. It was there, in his eyes; the man was unhinged. He must have left the party soon afterwards, knowing I was away from the cottage. He's completely paranoid, of course. He killed Beryl to stop her telling people he liked dressing in women's clothes.'

'That was it? No conspiracy? Just because he was ashamed? In this day and age, it's almost unbelievable.' Max squatted, to fill the dogs' bowls with steak from Libby's fridge. 'There you are, dogs. You two are heroes. Like Libby.'

22

WHISKY

The next evening, Libby leaned her elbows on the dinner table. 'What could be nicer than a few friends sharing a meal?' She smiled at each guest in turn. Max, Angela, Mandy and her boyfriend, Steve: they were all there, along with Owen, Angela's new man. It should have been a celebration, but her friend looked worried. 'What's wrong, Angela?'

Deep furrows showed on Angela's forehead. She gave a half-hearted smile and sat up straighter. 'I'm sorry. I was just thinking about George and Beryl. How many times did they share a meal over the years?'

'Or, at least, a drink,' put in Mandy with a wicked giggle. 'They'd known each other for ever.'

Libby spoke softly. 'Imagine having a secret, one so shocking that you couldn't bear your friends and neighbours to discover it.' She looked from one face to another. 'Your lifelong friend knows your secret, and she keeps it safely. Maybe she's known it for years and never told anyone. You'd think it would bring you closer together, but it had the opposite effect. George didn't feel secure at all.'

Max joined in. 'Then, the friend's life turns upside down, she's fired from her job, and the drinking gets out of hand.'

'George was convinced Beryl would give him away,' said Libby.

Angela mused aloud. 'He was devoted to Deirdre. He'd hidden his feelings from her for years.'

'Beryl's drink problem made it easy to poison her,' Libby pointed out. 'People visited her at home. It would be easy to slip something into a whisky bottle, or even give her one as a present. Why should anyone suspect George? It was Margery Halfstead who led me to the answer.'

Angela still frowned. 'We had a kind of conspiracy to keep Beryl's drinking quiet, because in a small town like this, public disgrace is one of the worst things that could happen.'

Owen's voice cut into the sombre mood. 'Is it always so exciting in Exham?'

Angela raised her glass to Libby. 'Ever since Libby came to live here, there's never been a dull moment. Not that it's her fault, of course.'

'I do sometimes feel as though I'm attracting trouble,' Libby admitted, 'but there seem to be pathetic characters like George Edwards everywhere, these days. Not to mention Ian Smith. Well done, Mandy, by the way. He got what he deserved. Are you going to press charges?'

Mandy took a swig of wine, smacking her lips in appreciation. 'No need. He won't be pinching women's bottom's again. In any case, the story's bound to get around to DCI Morrison. I wouldn't want to be in PC Ian Smith's shoes, with Gemma as a witness. I'll be surprised if he keeps his job.'

'I'd better make sure all the skeletons in my cupboard are well hidden, if I'm going to stick around with you people,' Owen said.

'Are you working in the area?' Libby asked.

Owen and Angela shared a glance, but before they could speak, Mandy interrupted. 'Owen's been looking at Exham for his latest venture.'

Libby puffed air through her lips. 'I hope you're not setting up another bakery. We'll have enough competition from Terence Marchant. I'm hoping the party gave him a nasty shock and showed him what he's up against. People here are very loyal.' She grinned. 'Especially after all that chocolate and wine. What an evening!'

'Go on, tell her,' Mandy pleaded.

Libby looked from her to Angela. 'What are you all grinning about? You're up to something. Come on, don't keep me in suspense.'

'To cut a long story short,' Owen said, 'I've known Terence for years. He's a pretty unsavoury character, with a tendency to over-reach himself. When he heard about your party, with everyone in town supporting you, he got cold feet over the new shop.'

Libby's pulse quickened. 'You mean, he's not going to open?'

Owen shook his head. 'Better than that. I offered to buy his business premises from him, and I've got an offer for you. How would you like the bakery, and your chocolates, to expand using those premises, and including a café?'

Libby gave her head a shake, trying to make sense of what she was hearing. 'You mean, buy Frank out? He'd never agree. Brown's Bakery is his life's work.'

'On the contrary. He wants to retire – apparently, he's been thinking about it for months, but he didn't know how to tell you, because of all the work you put into growing the bakery.'

'Am I that scary?'

Max raised an eyebrow. 'Terrifying. But the point is, Owen's offering to make the business viable in the long term.'

Libby turned to Mandy. 'What do you think?'

'I think it would be wonderful. We've been moaning about the size of the shop. It's a squash when all the customers are in at lunchtime. Here's the perfect opportunity to move out into a bigger space, still in the middle of Exham.'

Libby hesitated, tapping her finger on the table. 'I don't think I could run a café. I wouldn't have time, for one thing. I want to concentrate on the investigating, and we're about to get married.'

'Actually, Owen has another idea that takes care of that problem,' Angela said. Libby looked up, surprised, but her friend refused to meet her gaze.

Instead, Owen said, 'Angela's keen to take on that part of the business. She'll run the café for me.'

Libby's jaw hung open as her mind raced. 'That's – that's a brilliant idea. You'd be perfect. You're the best organiser in town.' She peered at Angela's face. 'You used the wine and chocolate event for practice, didn't you?' Her friend turned puce. 'Come on, admit it!'

Angela fiddled with a spoon on the table. 'It seemed a good opportunity for a dry run. See if I could cope.'

Mandy scoffed. 'Can't think of anyone who'd cope better. You can keep us organised – Mrs F's always forgetting to order ingredients.'

Libby tried to scowl. 'Thanks very much, young Mandy. You're right, though. I've been taking on far too much. This could be the answer to my worries.'

The friends spent hours planning the café until they were all too tired to talk any more.

As Libby and Max waved them off, full of tasty food and some of the best wine from Max's cellar, he took her hand, pulled her close and enveloped her in one of his wonderful bear hugs. 'Now. What about this wedding?'

Libby thought for a moment. 'When Bear was lost, I thought we ought to put it off – we wouldn't want to go ahead without him. But, now he's back, let's do it next week – but we'll keep it quiet.'

'Just us, our sons and their wives, Shipley and, of course, Bear. Perfect.'

23

MADEIRA CAKE

Sick with excitement, Margery drove William home from the hospital. It was the first time he'd ever agreed to be her passenger. He always insisted on driving. 'It's my job to look after you,' he'd said. Well, things were going to be a little different, now.

She chattered happily. As so often, William let her talk. 'You know Libby Forest, who found out George Edwards was the murderer?'

'Yes, dear.'

'Well, her missing dog turned up, out of the blue, the other evening.'

He grunted.

She went on, 'Turns out it escaped and walked all the way home. What do you think about that?'

'About what?'

'The dog coming home, all by himself.'

William muttered, 'Good for him.'

'You can trust a dog,' Margery said. 'By the way, why did you let Jason Franklin do the talking over the castle's speaking tube?'

She gave a secret smile at William's sharp intake of breath. 'He – er – he won it in a competition I organised. An essay.'

Margery snorted. 'Nonsense. You fixed it. Come on, William. Time to tell the truth. We've seen what happens when people keep secrets. Just so I know, what did you want from Franklin senior?'

She felt, rather than saw, William's sideways look. 'Planning permission,' he muttered. 'For that extension you set your heart on. I know the local planners will kick up a fuss and the neighbours will object. I thought I'd get the MP on our side before we start. Planners have to listen to the MP, don't they?'

Margery fell silent, her mind working feverishly. 'You were talking to Mr Franklin that day at the castle, weren't you, when you left me with the students? Sucking up to him? Telling him the boys were there, and you'd given his son a starring role?'

William turned his head away, but not before she caught a glimpse of heightened colour. 'I never should have got involved with that Thomas Franklin. You see, he suggested a payment to get our planning application through. Just a small one. He said it was common practice to grease the wheels, that's what he called it.'

He shot a quick glance at Margery. 'I paid him what he asked, but then he started demanding more and more. I had to give him half the money I'd saved. I'm not even sure there's enough left for the building work. I tried to stop, told him I wouldn't bother with the extension, but he turned nasty. He even threatened to tell everyone it was me who weighted the scales at the fishing competition.'

Tears filled his eyes. 'But it was George Edwards. I've been sure of it all the time. I wasn't surprised it was George who killed Beryl. I've never trusted him, since that fishing competition, but now I know he attacked you as well.'

His hands were clenched tight. 'I'm sure Franklin knew it too. He was probably getting money from George, too. He's a bad man, is Franklin, but he's so powerful...'

'Not so powerful he can escape the law.' Margery's voice rose in anger. Really, William could be heart-breakingly naïve. 'He's the one who'll be in trouble once the police know he's been extorting money from you.'

'But everyone will know I've been dishonest.'

'Who cares what people know? You're nothing of the sort at heart. We'll go to the police station tomorrow and explain everything. I'll bet it's not the first time that man's taken bribes. I expect the police will give you a good talking to, but he's the one who'll be in trouble. I feel sorry for his son.' She stopped talking. 'What?'

William's mouth hung open. He seemed to be gazing at his wife with new-found admiration. She rather liked it. 'Didn't you realise you were a suspect in Beryl's murder?'

His shoulders moved in a tiny shrug. 'I was hoping for the best. My head was in a spin, and they couldn't accuse me of attacking you, could they? I was in hospital.'

Margery touched his fingers. They felt cold. 'You silly old fool,' she said, but her voice was warm. 'Why don't you forget all about that extension? You never wanted it. You were organising it to make me happy, and I don't need it now.'

'You don't?' He sounded puzzled, confused.

Margery thought of the little box in his shed, full of memories, out of sight so as not to upset her. She sighed. Her husband was a stick-in-the mud and naïve, as well, getting caught up in a shady business he didn't properly understand. She smiled her secret smile once more. It no longer mattered that Father never approved of William. Margery loved her husband, and he returned her feelings. How could she ever have thought he was interested in that Annabel? Once they'd confessed everything to the police, she would keep her husband on the straight and narrow.

Her voice was matter-of-fact. 'An extension would be just another room to clean, anyway.'

'Good old Margery,' William muttered.

She tapped her husband's dear, familiar hand, and then let it go so she could steer the car neatly onto their drive. 'Now, let's get inside and have a nice cup of tea and a slice of Libby Forest's Madeira cake.'

ACKNOWLEDGEMENT

One of the pleasures of writing stories set in Somerset is the excuse to research the wonderful locations across the county that appear in my books.

My visits to Dunster Castle have been a real treat. If you're ever in Somerset, I'd recommend a visit, although a single trip doesn't allow nearly enough time to absorb the whole of this fascinating building, from the Victorian kitchen and servants' quarters that feature in my story, to the secret priest's hole in one of the bedrooms.

I would like to make it clear that each character in Murder at the Castle is entirely fictitious, and bears no resemblance whatever to any person, living or dead.

I count myself lucky to have had readers and reviewers who gave their time so generously to help with reading, revising and editing this book. I've received useful comments from Pippa Dunbar, Nick Evesham, Barbara Jensen, Kate McCormick, Doreen Pechey, Mary Robinson, Susan Schuman, and Frank Wright, and I'd like to thank them all for their time, trouble, eagle eyes and kind support.

A special thank you is also due to Caroline Ridding and Rose Fox from Boldwood Books, and to Wendy Janes, for the part they all played in editing and production.

As ever, I claim full responsibility for any errors remaining within the text.

Finally, a big thank you to my husband for all his help, especially with computer issues, tea, sympathy and encouragement.

MORE FROM FRANCES EVESHAM

We hope you enjoyed reading *Murder at the Castle*. If you did, please leave a review.

If you'd like to gift a copy, this book is also available as an ebook, digital audio download and audiobook CD.

Sign up to become a Frances Evesham VIP and receive a free copy of the Exham-on-Sea Kitchen Cheat Sheet. You will also receive news, competitions and updates on future books:

https://bit.ly/FrancesEveshamSignUp

ALSO BY FRANCES EVESHAM

The Exham-On-Sea Murder Mysteries

Murder at the Lighthouse

Murder on the Levels

Murder on the Tor

Murder at the Cathedral

Murder at the Bridge

Murder at the Castle

Murder at the Gorge

The Ham-Hill Murder Mysteries

A Village Murder

ABOUT THE AUTHOR

Frances Evesham is the author of the hugely successful Exham-on-Sea Murder Mysteries set in her home county of Somerset. In her spare time, she collects poison recipes and other ways of dispatching her unfortunate victims. She likes to cook with a glass of wine in one hand and a bunch of chillies in the other, her head full of murder—fictional only.

Visit Frances' website: https://francesevesham.com/

Follow Frances on social media:

twitter.com/francesevesham

facebook.com/frances.evesham.writer

bookbub.com/authors/frances-evesham

instagram.com/francesevesham

ABOUT BOLDWOOD BOOKS

Boldwood Books is a fiction publishing company seeking out the best stories from around the world.

Find out more at www.boldwoodbooks.com

Sign up to the Book and Tonic newsletter for news, offers and competitions from Boldwood Books!

http://www.bit.ly/bookandtonic

We'd love to hear from you, follow us on social media:

facebook.com/BookandTonic

twitter.com/BoldwoodBooks

instagram.com/BookandTonic